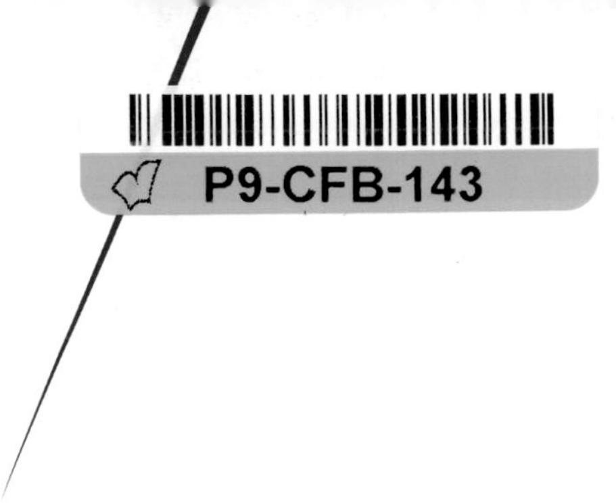

A SLAP IN THE FACE

THE
SEAGULL
LIBRARY OF
GERMAN
LITERATURE

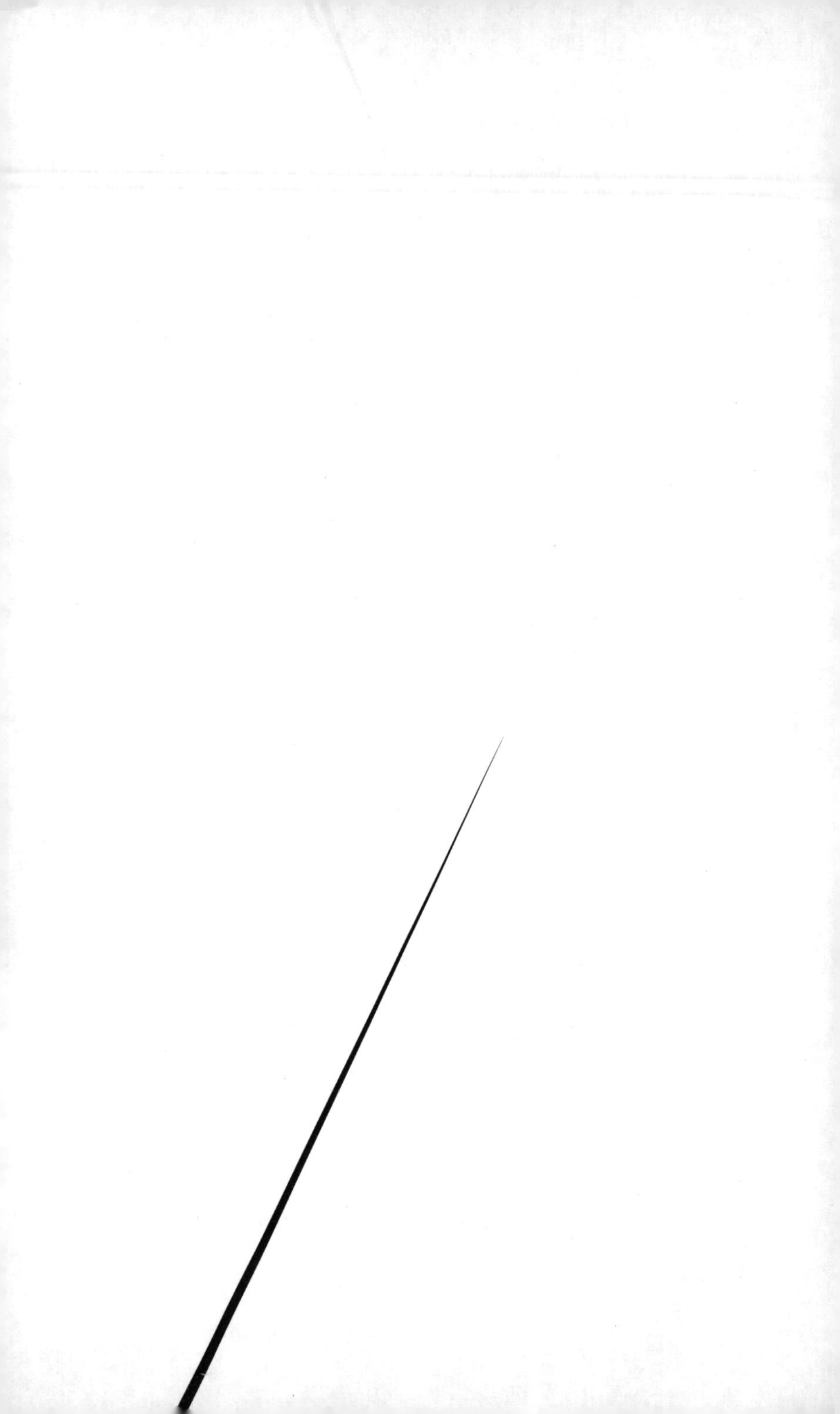

ABBAS KHIDER

A SLAP IN THE FACE

Translated by Simon Pare

LONDON NEW YORK CALCUTTA

This publication has been supported by a grant from
the Goethe-Institut India

Seagull Books, 2022

First published in German as *Ohrfeige* by Abbas Khider

First published in English translation by Seagull Books, 2018

Published as part of the Seagull Library of German Literature, 2022

ISBN 978 1 8030 9 000 9

British Library Cataloguing-in-Publication Data
A catalogue record for this book is available from the British Library

Typeset by Seagull Books, Calcutta, India
Printed and bound by WordsWorth India, New Delhi, India

For Orfeas

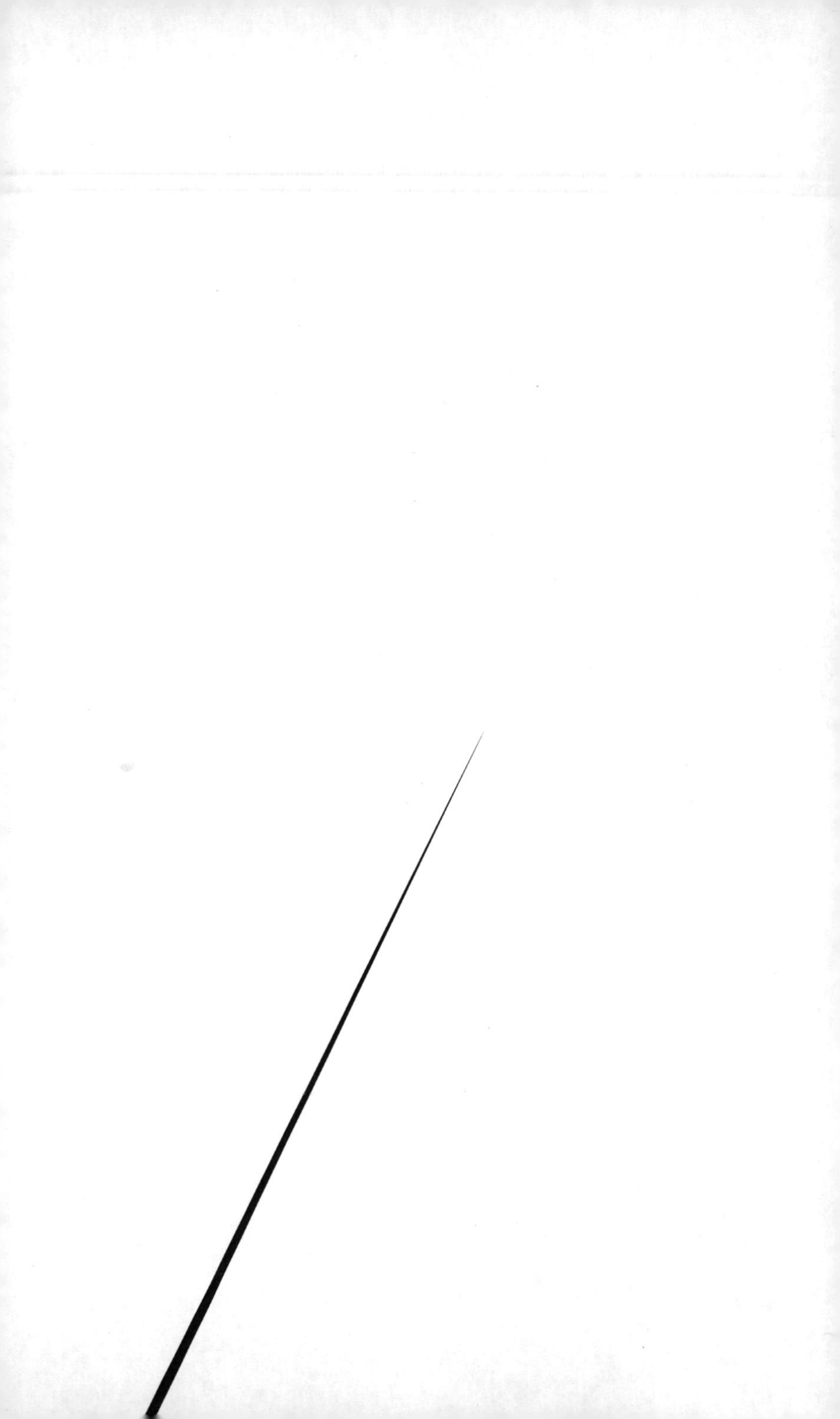

She sits there, stiff and speechless on her revolving chair, as if the slap has left her numb.

'You are quiet and sit still!'

I reach for the gaffer tape in my jacket pocket and strap her hands to the armrests and her ankles to the bottom of the chair. I stick several strips over her red-painted lips.

'I want hear nothing!'

Slowly I begin to relax. I sit down on the guest chair opposite her, take a piece of paper from her desk, sprinkle a little hash into my tobacco and roll myself a cigarette. I light it and take a long drag, relishing it.

The paper gives off a burnt taste, and at first I feel like retching but I force myself to enjoy this special cigarette. I draw on it as if trying to suck out the contents, inhale the smoke deep into my lungs and savour the slight stinging sensation in my chest. I feel more alive than I've felt for a long time.

I stand up, lean forward, move closer and blow the smoke in her face several times. Since her mouth is taped up, she's forced to breathe in the smoke through her nose. She tries to turn her head away and wheezes so hard that the tape bulges out and then in again. It feels amazingly good to smoke a joint in a government building.

'We going to talk, *Frau* Schulz. I wanted to always, and you have no time or will for me when I waiting outside your room. But this is it! If you want or not, now we talk. But German is hard for me and I want tell many things. I must speak Arabic with you so I can speak free. Sorry!'

I don't want to struggle through German any more, through this jungle of cases and articles you can never remember. Of course it's stupid to speak Arabic with her now, but what the hell. Even if Arabic were her mother tongue, she still wouldn't understand me. She comes from a completely different world to me. An earthling is currently speaking to a Martian—or the other way around.

This feels more like a Christian confession, a concept someone once explained to me. You sit on a chair in a room that's far too small. Anyway, now I can talk and unburden my soul of its worries.

So, to my first question: What's your name?

Are you a Sabine or an Anne-Marie? Maybe this is an Astrid sitting opposite me? Or should I call you Inge? Oh, I almost forgot that you can't answer me. You can nod though, can't you? Well, nod if I get it right. Anita? Katharina? Ursula?

Surnames create such distance between people. It's interesting to give someone like you a first name all of a sudden. It's like giving God a name. Allah would be less intimidating if he had a first name. Amir Allah or Wilma Allah sounds a lot friendlier, don't you think?

You, *Frau* Schulz, are one of those who decide how I may or should live. Imagine for a second that you were in my position. Wouldn't you want to know what this godlike figure's first name was? The person with the power to make your life heaven or hell.

If you could only see yourself right now!

A few minutes ago you were safely ensconced behind your desk, the flat screen like a shield in front of your face and your torso protected by mountains of files. You kept waving your sharp-nibbed fountain pen around in the air as if you were stabbing flies, crushing people's hopes with the weight of your oversized stamp. It would come crashing down on your desk like a judge's gavel.

And now? Here you are. Helpless. All trussed up like a parcel. Sitting there in your expensive black leather chair. You were a goddess, a force of nature, exercising your authority over other people. I was at your mercy, but like a mythical hero I have risen up and stormed Olympus. And soon I'll leave you to your tiny pen-pusher's office again. You'll be left sitting here, as lonely as a creator whose creatures have forgotten him. A god without believers doesn't exist. That's true of goddesses too. I'll leave you behind and go away to a distant land.

You know full well who I am. I'm one of the many whose files you've read and examined, only to set them aside again.

My name's Karim Mensy. How do you do.

Another one of those hard-to-remember foreign names. For you I was asylum seeker 3873 or something. Worth no more than the numbers I had to take, and then sit and wait. It was a pointless wait, which I only put up with because I hoped I'd be understood and given a chance. Instead, I kept being sent away. I know your sayings off by heart: Please bring another certificate. And I always had to wait, even in my dreams at night. I've even waited to get a queue number here! Look, I've still got it in my pocket.

I could tell from your expression that you didn't remember me when I marched in here a minute ago. No wonder, given how much I've changed over the past few years. I used to be chubby and my chin was unshaven. As you can see, I don't have a beard any more. It would be daft to go about wearing a bush like Osama bin Laden's after 9/11. Since then, all Arabic men walk around with cheeks as clean-shaven as a baby's bum. And look how baggy my clothes are now. Labouring on a building site's the best way to lose weight.

My intention in coming to see you today was simply to chat with you for a while, one-to-one. What about? I'm not really sure myself. I actually meant to pay you a visit three weeks ago. I wanted to travel from Munich to Niederhofen an der Donau one last time before I have to leave Germany for ever. To say goodbye to my friends—and to you, *Frau* Schulz. It was a Friday. As usual the police were circling around Munich station like vultures scavenging for rotten meat. They were marching up and down in their khaki uniforms, scrutinizing the face of every passer-by.

My friend Salim spent a long time over by the big departures board on the main station concourse, watching the pigs for me and constantly ringing me with updates about the situation on the platforms.

Time was racing by, and it was only fifteen minutes until my train was due to leave. I don't know which was worse—my fear of missing the train, or my fear of being arrested just before I reached my train. In any case, I'd chosen a perfect position. Mongdratzerl, a Bavarian restaurant, is right in the centre of the concourse and has an exit leading out to Arnulfstrasse on the northern side of the station. I could keep one eye on the concourse and the other on the street outside. I could have done a runner at the slightest sign of danger.

My phone rang again, cutting through my thoughts. 'It's me,' said Salim. 'My God, it's like the fuzz know you're here. They just won't leave the platform.

They're wandering up and down like wind-up toy robots.'

On the table in front of me was a cup of coffee and half a glass of water. My rucksack was lying under a chair. I leafed distractedly through the *Süddeutsche Zeitung*, stopping only to stare at the occasional headline. Like a detective in one of those old films, I was holding it so high that it shielded my entire face. I would lower it at regular intervals, apparently by chance, so that I could just about peek over. I had to keep a constant eye on my surroundings so that I would notice in good time if anyone was heading towards me. I jumped every time the waitress sidled up and suddenly appeared beside me to ask if everything was to my satisfaction.

Disguising myself as a reader has worked at many other stations. The police generally take no notice of me. They obviously think that an illegal immigrant from one of those underdeveloped countries won't be able to read. Holding the *Süddeutsche Zeitung* is pretty good camouflage for an illegal immigrant in Bavaria.

Oh, *Frau* Schulz, that reminds me of my language course here in Niederhofen. Our teacher, *Frau* Müllerschön, recommended that we read the newspaper every day. We should start off with a tabloid like *BILD* because the sentences were easy to understand, but as soon as we began to notice the many grammatical mistakes, we should move on to a broadsheet like the *Süddeutsche*. I never detected any linguistic howlers in *BILD*; I found it perfect for learning German. At some point, however, I was forced to switch to the *Süddeutsche Zeitung*, although I still have trouble understanding their articles. First, I felt a bit embarrassed toting *BILD* around with me because of its lousy reputation; and second, I realized that, whether they're sitting on a local train, at work or in a cafe, the kind of people I know don't read papers like the *Süddeutsche*. They flick through tabloids which have lots of pictures of jaw-droppingly attractive naked women and men instead of articles.

So I got used to the *SZ*—or at least to hiding behind it and pretending to be absorbed. I act the part of the inquisitive citizen, and people seem to buy it. The pigs would never bother a patron in a cafe or bar who's reading an intelligent newspaper. None of the countless policemen I've met in the past few months would ever dream of asking me to show my papers in a situation like that. Keep up appearances and live up to people's expectations and you're completely safe in Munich.

Then, through the restaurant's glass door I caught sight of some red-shirted Bayern Munich fans outside on the concourse. They looked drunk and were running towards the underground station, roaring and laughing. Two policemen were tailing the group like wolves stalking their prey, but instead of pouncing, one of the officers disappeared into a tobacconist's. Meanwhile, his colleague studied a few long-haired boys and girls lounging around in front of a bookshop in their ripped jeans and anarchist T-shirts amid rucksacks and musical instruments. From inside the cafe I could hear the policeman yelling, 'Get up right now! Go and sit in the waiting room like decent citizens! Stop lazing around outside the shops!'

Another bunch of Bayern fans walked past, their singing and bellowing even louder than the previous group's. The punks struggled to their feet. Having initially acted with exaggerated self-assurance and indifference, one of the girls became flustered and quickly gathered her stuff. She was draped with all kinds of jewellery, her hair shimmered in at least five different colours, and she looked like a frayed Christmas tree. As she was getting to her feet, the policeman suddenly grabbed her wrist and twisted her arm behind her back. The young woman clenched her fingers frantically into a fist, but the policeman slowly peeled her fingers apart until she finally gave in. She must have been hiding something in her hand because she was led away soon afterwards. When the football fans noticed this, they staggered over to the police officers and started having a go at them, waving their beer cans around in the air. By now the second policeman had reappeared from the tobacconist's and drawing himself up to his full height, drove the fans back as if he were not alone but one of a hundred shield-bearing officers at a demonstration. The fans stood their ground and began to shout, so he took out his radio and obviously called for reinforcements. The little punk took advantage of the momentary confusion to break free and run away. One of the policemen chased after her, cursing, while the other had his hands full dealing with the Bayern fans.

This was my opportunity. Just then my mobile rang again. Salim's voice cracked. 'Your train's here! Come on, get moving! Platform twenty-four!'

I'd settled the bill with the dirndl-wearing waitress straight after ordering, so I was able immediately to jump up and run. Anywhere else a sprinting foreigner would arouse suspicion, but everyone dashes around stations as if someone's chasing them. A sea of faces flashed past me: white, ruddy, brown, black and yellow ones; sad, smiling, lost and waiting ones; long, round, wide, hairy, smooth, pale, bloody . . . Everyone looked threatening to me, even the foreigners selling sandwiches and drinks in the many snack bars. I felt under surveillance, sure that at any moment someone was going to overpower me from behind and knock me to the ground.

At last I caught sight of Salim, who had worn nothing but black clothes in mourning since his mother's death the previous year. He was standing on the platform but he wasn't alone: two men in civilian clothing were checking his papers. Still sprinting, I changed course and raced past the platform as if I were scared I was going to miss my underground train. I didn't dare look back from the top of the escalator as it carried me slowly down into the depths.

I wanted to pay you a visit much earlier, *Frau* Schulz, but unfortunately things kept cropping up. That's probably a good thing in hindsight. If I had caught my train, I might never have reached my destination. Those local trains stop at just about every tiny village. Often police officers get on, and of course they never ask any of the good-looking blond passengers for ID every bloody time they go through the train checking tickets. They head straight for me or some other dark-haired or otherwise foreign-looking passenger. Foreigners should avoid taking German trains on principle. The only safe option is first class on an InterCity Express because the police seldom show their faces there. Unfortunately, the ticket costs a fortune, as does the matching Hugo Boss shirt you need for camouflage.

People are constantly getting on and off slow trains. At first I wanted to get to know some locals, so I was happy whenever someone sat down beside me. I would often sit down next to a fair-haired person on a bus or train myself and try to engage him in conversation. I saw it as part of cultural exchange, and it helped me to learn the language. Recently, however, I've increasingly shied away from contact with other people, preferring to keep to myself. I'm fed up with talking about subjects of no relevance to my present life. The constant enquiries about the past are killing me. For months now I've taken pains to avoid any news from home, listening and reading about it once a week at most, and as superficially as possible. Only the headlines, so I'm not overwhelmed with melancholy. German passengers don't want to talk to me about anything else, though. Always the same questions: Where are you from? When are you going back? 9/11 was horrible, wouldn't you agree? Do Arabs actually know what democracy is? Are you a Muslim? What do you think about what the Americans have done to your country? Do you see them as liberators or occupiers? Is life better now the dictatorship is over? What do you think: will democracy work over there?

No one ever contemplates what my life might be like now. The difficulty of getting a residence permit, the torment at the foreigners' registration office, the harassment by the federal crime agency, the embarrassment caused by the intelligence services or the trivial details of constitutional protection. And why doesn't anyone notice police racism? How does not being able to live in my homeland or abroad affect me? *Frau* Schulz?

I didn't use to be this bitter, but the experiences of recent years have changed me. The police in particular get me down. Bloody cops! Only a few hours more, and those scumbags will hopefully never see my face again. I have to get out of this country!

I've already found a smuggler to take me to Finland. As far as I know, the Finns have no specific agreements with other European countries, which means they don't exchange photos or fingerprints with Germany. So I'll be able to make a fresh request for asylum there and start a new life.

For the past few months, I've done nothing but get ready for my trip. I've worked illegally from dawn till dusk on a building site for a Greek boss. Every day I've hauled stones, metal and pipes to save up the 3,500 euros the people smuggler demanded for his services. I gave him one thousand euros as a deposit last week. He'll use it to get me a fake passport. I hope he's not taking me for a ride. At least I know the cafe where he kills time and works. People call him Abu Salwan. He's picking me up tonight at midnight, and then we'll be off. He won't get the rest of the agreed sum immediately, though. Salim has it, and he's only allowed to give the cash to Abu Salwan when I've reached Finland. I'll ring him from there to confirm my arrival. That's the deal.

It isn't at all hard to find people like my Greek boss or my smuggler. There are lots of middlemen in Munich organizing these kinds of meetings between 'customers' and 'suppliers'. You soon find out where they hang out if you're an illegal immigrant or an asylum seeker. You can't just go along and enquire about their services, though. You have to get hold of someone who knows them, as a precaution.

The people who deal with Iraqis sit in the Al Nurr mosque every evening. People like us simply call it the 'Goethe Mosque' because it's in Goethestrasse.

It's not like how one might imagine a mosque to be, furnished with a towering minaret, ornate carpets and historical frescoes. This one has a single large, bare room on the third floor of a six-storey building.

These middlemen spend the daytime elsewhere, at the Enlil Cultural Centre which is in the same building. I have no idea who came up with that name. Enlil is a Sumerian god. 'En' means 'lord' and 'lil' means 'wind', thus 'Lord of the Wind'. The first time I entered the meeting room, it reminded me less of an ancient Mesopotamian temple than of a greasy spoon near the North Gate in the centre of Baghdad. More specifically, I thought of the area around the Scheherazade cinema where thieves, alcoholics and homeless people hang out.

The room is on the first floor and has one large window, which lets in no light due to the seven- or eight-storey Goethe Hotel on the other side of the street. Blue and white tables, plastic chairs, a fridge stocked with soft drinks, a TV tuned to Al Jazeera round the clock, and lastly a corner where you can order shishas, tea and drinks. At the back are toilets, the kitchen and a barber's shop. There's a large picture of the Freedom Statue in central Baghdad.

There are a lot of foreign supermarkets, cafes, food stands, restaurants and small grocer's shops near Munich's main railway station, along with countless clubs for various ethnic groups. There are Kurds, Turkmens, Christians, Shiite and Sunni Muslims and other Iraqi minorities, as well as Persians, Turks and

Pakistanis. Most of them gather in and around Goethestrasse.

None of these cultural societies in the West-Eastern Divan area actually engage in any cultural activities. At best, one can see one of these centres as a kind of cafe or club where people drink tea, smoke shishas and play dominoes, cards or backgammon. It's claimed that the owners of these tearooms and card clubs founded the societies for tax purposes. They're sham cultural societies. No books, magazines or newspapers. They organize no readings or any other events. Just a few men sitting around together, their loud, nervous chatter like warning shouts from soldiers on the front line. Yet many things about these places are invaluable to people like us—far more important than books. The German words 'Kultur' and 'Goethe' sound like superfluous luxuries in comparison.

I found my job on the building site through a middleman at the Enlil Centre, and I first caught sight of my smuggler sitting under the picture of the Iraqi Freedom Statue in the barbershop. A guy with several gold chains around his neck: a Kurdish Christian from Erbil in northern Iraq. He finds his clients in the various clubs or at the Goethe Mosque. The smugglers offer everything an Iraqi in Munich—and probably in the whole of Bavaria—urgently needs: black-market job announcements, details about applying for asylum, work and residence permits, information about specialist immigration lawyers, people who arrange marriages of convenience, matchmakers between girls from back home and Iraqis living in Germany, and a money transfer office.

These services aren't free, of course. They are businessmen who know how to turn worthless sand into money. They speak Bavarian and they've already solved every problem under the sun. Most of them are married to German women. No one really knows how they establish and maintain their contacts with local businessmen. Each works on his own and cultivates his own network. My job fixer, Abu Layla, is supposedly one of the most influential men in his field, among other reasons because he speaks flawless Turkish, Greek and German, allowing him to use his links to the three largest ethnic groups in Bavaria. He demanded four hundred euros out of my first wages to set me up with a job. Nothing was written down, and Salim was our witness. People claim that the employers also pay Abu Layla something for his fixing, but I have no idea how much.

My Greek boss, Kostas, gave me my dough punctually at the end of every month. Everyone usually complains about their bosses on the black market. I heard of other businessmen refusing to pay the full wage or keeping their employees waiting for their money for months, but Kostas was a decent man. I had to change building sites with him on a weekly basis to make sure that employment inspectors wouldn't catch us. His team was mainly made up of Turks and Greeks. Sometimes other illegal workers would join us for short periods; often they were Poles, Persians, Pakistanis, Kurds or Arabs. He 'employed' me for several months. He kept me on because I would do anything he asked without any backchat. Roaring with laughter, he would call me an 'Arab donkey' when he occasionally drank *raki* during the lunch break with his more trusted workers, of which I was soon one.

I always eventually found a solution to even the thorniest issues at the Enlil Centre. Without the Lord of the Wind, my life would have turned out completely differently. And that was true of many others who, like me, sought a fresh start there. Take Salim's brother Majed for example, who now works as a mechanic for BMW and has been living in Munich's Freimann neighbourhood for the past few years. He found his wife through the centre. As he once confided to Salim and me, he was quickly brassed off with the 'European Evas': 'They don't cook, they don't clean, but they still want their husbands to treat them like queens and they walk around in skirts that are far too short, even in January when it's minus twenty. You find them dancing with other men on the platform at the disco at weekends. They're constantly having affairs, and yet they expect unconditional respect. What is this place?'

So Majed ordered himself a girl on the marriage market from back home. The matchmaker showed him several photos of young women, all of whom could cook and clean and shared Majed's conception of marriage. Next, Majed rang his mother in Baghdad, who had also received a copy of the brochure containing the women's photos. She selected one particular bride, paid her a personal visit and was soon enthused. Majed's mother said she was a virgin and that her legs were neither too short nor too long.

'Women like her bear healthy children,' she claimed. She said that the girl had fleshy heels, which meant that her vagina was tight, promising more intense pleasure for her husband. She rubbed her thighs together when she walked, which signalled that no man had yet mounted her; if they had, her legs would bend outwards. Her face was round: 'a sign of honour!' Her nose was straight: 'the countenance of a true Babylonian thoroughbred! What more could you want, my son?'

The girl with the fleshy heels had a long way to go to obtain a German residence permit. First, she was smuggled north to the Kurds, and from there into Turkey. Majed visited her in Istanbul and married her there. Of course the girl hadn't made the journey alone; her brother was escorting her. He explained to Majed that he had no wish to go back to Iraq. So Majed had to help him out with some money to head to Athens. Majed, however, initially travelled back to Germany on his own, handed in the invitation, the marriage certificate and a load of other documents to the immigration agency and waited for four months until his wife was granted a visa and could finally fly to join him. The whole thing cost him just under twelve thousand deutschmarks, with five thousand going to the matchmaker who'd done the arranging and organized the bride's illegal journey to Istanbul with her chaperone.

Salim is very fond of his brother's wife. Her name is Fatima and she seems generally content—not necessarily with her ageing and jealous husband, but certainly with their children.

Majed is one of many to have got married in this way. There were countless such ventures during the embargo on Iraq. Iraqi fathers and mothers who couldn't earn enough to feed their families married off one girl abroad so that the other children might survive. It is rumoured that Iraqi army officers were also mixed up in schemes exploiting these desperate people.

I have also heard that many Iraqi girls were sold off to Iran, where they were made available for 'marriages of pleasure'. Iran, like most Shiite communities, allows this form of temporary marriage. In a 'marriage for pleasure' a man 'marries' a woman for a period of his choosing, which can be as little as half an hour.

Other girls were taken from Iraq and sold to Saudis. Marriages of pleasure don't exist in Saudi Arabia, but the rich and powerful have slave quarters in their palaces. Those men aren't interested exclusively in girls, but in pretty boys and transsexuals too. The southern Iraqi city of Basra is allegedly a hub for influential traders in this kind of 'goods'. I had heard repeated reports of young people being sold by their families, but it was only when I came across the Cafe Enlil in Munich that I found out exactly how the business operated and how well organized it was.

The marriage market has changed since the fall of Saddam. Expatriates can now travel to Iraq to choose their future wives for themselves. Yet there are still matchmakers at the Cafe Enlil for men with no relatives back home and who are intent on finding an Iraqi wife. However, the matchmakers have widened their portfolios and will now listen to other kinds of requests. Business continues as usual: there is always fixing to be done.

If it weren't for those crooks, *Frau* Schulz, I'd have gone mad long ago and got nowhere; I would have given up any slim hope of some day and somewhere finding a new homeland of my choosing. Enlil offers a way out of the labyrinth of exile.

For instance, money transfers to Iraq work flawlessly. You hand some cash to an intermediary in Munich and he has it delivered to your family home in Baghdad. You do have to pay ten to fifteen per cent commission for this service, but it's impossible to transfer money via any of the usual channels. There are no current accounts and no official Western Union branches in Iraq. Western Union has headquarters everywhere else and is the most important address on the planet for refugees and traffickers, but it charges exorbitant interest rates to send money to Iraq. Its representatives there are dubious travel agency owners who cannot be trusted. Work with them and you might never see your money again—and there's no possibility of a refund.

Some weeks ago, I finally had a bit of money over to send to my family—five hundred euros. Someone at Enlil referred me to a man I subsequently met at the mosque. He took the money, somehow spirited it halfway around the world and within a few days his brother appeared at my family home in Baghdad and sat down in our living room. Then he handed over the precise amount, minus the agreed commission. My father called me to confirm that he'd received the money.

So many weird problems and puzzles arise in exile that a normal person could never imagine. All kinds of difficulties strike you as suddenly and unexpectedly as a natural disaster. We are utterly defenceless. We need the middlemen, the mafiosi, the money-grubbers, the smugglers and the corrupt policemen and officials if we're to survive and not go completely mad; we need all the bloodsuckers seeking to profit from our situation. We need them far more than we need all the staff members of Amnesty International put together.

I have spent the past few months in constant fear of the police because I no longer have a residence permit, *Frau* Schulz. I left the house only to go to work; otherwise I hid at home. Munich seemed like one big prison and the city's inhabitants like my unyielding guards. The police constantly hassle me, whether my papers are valid or not. Ever since I set foot in this country, I have had to keep my eyes peeled and I avoid places like railway stations and pedestrian zones whenever possible. The security forces in those places are always on the lookout for black-haired, dark-skinned people, whether they're harmless students or drug-dealing criminals. Maybe there's a competition between police officers. Maybe they keep a league table of who has stopped the most black-haired people and arrested the most refugees, and the winner gets a pair of golden handcuffs or an all-expenses-paid trip to Morocco.

I was stopped virtually every day during my early days in Niederhofen—on the street, in the pedestrian zone, at the main station, and never for any obvious reason. Every time a police officer caught sight of me he would ask me to show my papers. Within a few weeks I was known to every police officer in town, and from then on they generally left me in peace. Some of them were even friendly and would say hello to me.

One day last spring, I noticed two new policemen on the beat together. They were strutting through the pedestrian zone, pounding the concrete with their powerful strides, as if they were magnificently plumed fighting cocks amid frail white battery chickens. No sooner had they spotted me than they headed straight towards me and asked to see my papers. Before I could react, one of the usual cops called out from the other side of the street, 'Leave him alone. We know him!' Proud of this small victory, I flashed the two new police officers a smug grin. They didn't find it at all funny, but they let me go my way.

In time, my mate Rafid came up with a hilarious way of annoying the police. He would hand them his ID when they asked to see it, then start humming a variation of the Opus song, which soon got on the police officers' nerves.

Live is life
Na na na na na
La ba da ba ba live
Na na na na na
Black is black
Na na na na na
Black
Na na na na na
Schwarz is black
Na na na na na
La ba da ba ba black
Na na na na na
Dark is black
Na na na na na
Live

I never tested this method. I accepted the police as part of my inescapable fate. They clung to me like barnacles. I had no choice but to get used to them, regarding them as a familiar, recurring nightmare I no longer needed to fear. You can combat ghosts simply by refusing to take them seriously.

However, all the old nightmares have returned since my asylum application was revoked and my residence permit withdrawn, like those of so many other Iraqis since Saddam's fall. I'll never forget that day. I was lying on the couch in my flat in Niederhofen, waiting for a few friends to come around so we could go for a walk together. It was a Saturday. I got up to fetch the post. The letterbox was overflowing with promotional flyers and bills, but hidden among them was a green letter. I was immediately on edge. Green envelopes are always a sign of extremely important correspondence. They come from an omnipotent authority such as the Federal Office for Migration and Refugees or the foreigners' registration office. My heart was thumping like the pneumatic drill I would soon be using illegally on a construction site. Opening the letter, I found a very long text in German and Arabic—almost twenty pages long. The revocation of my asylum application. In a nutshell, they wished to inform me that the situation had improved in Iraq since the Americans had removed Saddam Hussein as dictator, and hence there was no longer any reason for me to remain in Germany. I was to return to my homeland straight away.

I spent the whole weekend in a daze. First thing on Monday morning I rushed to the Caritas office. There I met *Frau* Mohmadi, a nice woman married to an Egyptian who put her life on the line for us refugees. She advised me to consult a lawyer.

'You won't get far, of course, but you'll certainly gain a few months to move freely and weigh up your options. Your residence permit is going to expire soon. Your asylum passport will also be taken away from you. The best thing that could happen after that would be a stay of deportation, meaning you'll have to remain within twenty miles of Niederhofen. All of that is so they can eventually deport you.'

'But the letter is full of rubbish,' I said. 'There may no longer be a dictatorship in Iraq but it's still total chaos. Bombs are exploding every day. Armies from around the globe and loyalists to Saddam are shooting each other to bits. Terrorists are drawn to the country to join in with the fighting. Iraq isn't a state any more; it's the scene of a battle between the major powers and a bunch of fanatics. Even the Iraqis have no idea who's currently fighting whom in most of the attacks and skirmishes. And before you know it you're caught in the crossfire and end up as one of tens of thousands of collateral victims. I'm desperately trying to get my family out of the country, and now I'm meant to go back to that minefield? The German authorities might as well shoot me right here: then at least I won't have to wait until I'm torn apart by a bomb while shopping. No, why don't *you* shoot me, *Frau* Mohmadi? Come on, do it!'

'You said it yourself: none of those pen-pushers could care less. You know that. It's the Iraqis' turn now, just as it was the Yugoslavs' after the Balkan War. First they let them in, then after the war they send them back to the chaos without giving a second's thought to what will become of them. The same drama, over and over again. And whatever you say, you won't change that. Should I put you in touch with a lawyer?'

'Yes, please!'

'Leave the letter with me. I'll take it along. You don't necessarily have to be there if you don't want to be. It's pure routine. The lawyer contests the decision and gains you a little breathing space; that's the best he can do. It's his bread and butter. I'll call you to keep you posted. Is your mobile number still the same?'

'Yes.'

'And please, please, don't get any stupid ideas about leaving Germany on your current passport! You're banned from travelling since you received the revocation letter, and that includes other Schengen countries.'

She patted me sympathetically on the arm, and it was all I could do not to lay my head against her chest and cry my eyes out.

The lawyer did indeed buy me an extra two months. After that I was supposed to go to the foreigners' registration office. Come and see you, *Frau* Schulz. Hand in my blue asylum passport in exchange for a Stay of Deportation document. Lots of rumours were doing the rounds among Iraqis, though. Some claimed that your office would arrest us and place us in pre-deportation custody in Munich or Nuremberg.

No new prospects presented themselves until shortly before the two months ran out. The best thing would have been to marry a local woman and use her status to acquire a residence permit. I thought of my ex-lover Lada, who, though not German, was a quota refugee and therefore had a permanent residence permit. She hasn't been in touch, though, and she must still be married to Dimitri. I don't know of a single acquaintance who has actually married a young German woman to be able to stay here.

Another possibility would have been to conclude a sham marriage with an Eastern European girl holding a German passport. They're available via Russian sham marriage agents in Niederhofen, but I can't afford one. They charge upwards of twelve thousand euros and don't even give any guarantee that it'll really work out. Whatever the outcome, the money is gone.

My final alternative, therefore, is to clear off and try my luck in a different country. That's the option I've chosen.

So I didn't come to see you at the office after the two months had elapsed, *Frau* Schulz. I ran away to Munich and went underground. It's easier to hide in a big city than in a small town. I'm living with Salim. You know him. He was my roommate back at the asylum centre in Bayreuth, and we were both later sent here to Niederhofen. As soon as his residence permit came through, he moved to be near his brother in Munich and has worked in a restaurant ever since. He's lucky: his permit hasn't been revoked yet. He works 'normally' for a temping agency, and they found him a job in a restaurant.

It was Salim who first took me to the Goethe Mosque, and he also established the first contacts for me at the Enlil Cultural Centre. That's where I found my construction job with Kostas and also my smuggler, Abu Salwan. And today, *Frau* Schulz, he's going to help me to break free of my never-ending German ordeal.

A pride of big cats is hunting a herd of gazelles. Ants are marching across the screen as if on military parade. A butterfly flutters towards a flower and alights on it. Laughing dolphins swim with a woman in a burqa around a pool. People in Halloween costumes grieve in front of a carved pumpkin. A gull glides over the ocean, exploding bombs reflected in its eyes. A man stands in front of ruined buildings, calling, 'This is hell! A curse on democracy!' The White House sparkles as if it has been freshly polished. Fog over water. Letters rise up out of the sea like golden fish and assemble themselves into the word AL JAZEERA. *More words appear from the waves*: THE LATEST NEWS FROM AROUND THE WORLD. *Adverts immediately follow. A woman's lips in front of a mirror.* DAX COSMETICS, CASHMERE SECRET. *A voice purrs, 'A light foundation with a heavenly fragrance. For silky smooth skin.' Cut. A party somewhere. She's wearing a backless black dress. A handsome man greets her, leans forward and kisses her hand. She flounces over to her friends by the bar. They stare at her face in amazement. Next advert. A baby smiles with glowing eyes at a bottle in its mother's hand.* NIDO FULL FAT MILK POWDER. ORIGINAL NESTLÉ.

I pick up the remote control and switch the TV to mute. My eyes pan to the half-smoked cigarette in the ashtray on the coffee table. I reach for the butt and light it.

'Life would be totally unbearable without hash, wouldn't it, Salim?'

Salim doesn't reply. The sweet smell blends in with the aroma of biryani rice wafting through the flat. Is Salim cooking? Or am I so hungry, I'm already dreaming of tasty Iraqi dishes? Is Salim actually in the flat? Oh, I'm not going to get up and look for him. It's so comfy here on the sofa!

Three years and four months have passed since I came here with the help of a smuggler. Now I'm going to leave this country with the help of one of his fellows. Today, around midnight, he will pick me up and whisk me away. I'm like an unwanted advert that keeps being dropped into letterboxes, although there are stickers everywhere marked: STOP! NO ADVERTS PLEASE! LESS WASTE!

I have as little idea of how my future journey will turn out as you have interest in it, *Frau* Schulz. I don't know what Finland has in store for me, other than frost. And yet I'm incredibly excited. I'm looking forward to being able to start a new life somewhere else. After all, my relationship with their authorities is completely virginal.

I have lived here for years and now I'm leaving empty-handed. What I'm taking with me is embedded deep inside, including many memories of other lost souls and of how we fell into each other's arms so far from home.

When I arrived in Germany I thought I was in France because that's where my father had paid them to take me. He'd given a smuggler in Baghdad five thousand dollars to arrange my journey to Paris.

Uncle Murad, an old friend of my father's, would be waiting for me there and would then pay the smuggler another four thousand dollars upon receipt of the delivery, i.e. me. But things turned out very differently.

The trip didn't take long, something like five weeks, and went off almost without a hitch. A whole host of smugglers accompanied me through many different stages. From Baghdad we took the northern route by car to Istanbul. From there, all of us—six men, two women, three children and a new smuggler—travelled to the Greek border. We rowed in a dinghy across the border river, the Evros. A Greek then took over on the other side of the border and guided us to Athens, where our group split up. A new middleman escorted me north to Patras. There, an Italian hid me in the cab of his lorry. He steered the HGV on to a ferry and I woke up the following day in Venice. The next smuggler took me to Rome, where I was handed over to an Iraqi claiming to be half German and from Bielefeld. He left me for a few nights over New Year in an empty basement flat somewhere on the outskirts of the city. 2001 began with the two of us travelling by train to Bolzano in South Tyrol or, to give it its German name, Bozen. That same evening I was crouching with three other passengers in the back of a van. A five- or six-hour drive without any sense of direction. We were dropped off on a road somewhere in the small hours.

'You've made it! Hurry up and get out! The station's over there!'

No sooner had our feet hit the asphalt than the driver put his foot to the floor and was gone. Up to that point, there had always been a smuggler waiting for me, yet this time I found myself with three other blokes in an unknown place. None of us knew where we were or what to do next. We were standing on a deserted country road, surrounded by snow-covered fields, a few leafless trees and a chill that bit into our bone marrow. There was nobody and no cars to be seen, nothing but a couple of buildings far in the distance.

'Is this Germany?' one of the lads asked.

'More like France,' I said, despite having nothing much to go on.

'Oh no! We paid our way to Munich!'

'And I paid to Paris!'

One of the others interrupted our argument.

'If we hang around here like idiots, it won't matter where we are because someone's going to spot us!'

At this the three lads rushed off towards the houses where the station was supposed to be, leaving me standing there. I too moved away from the road and hid behind a tree. I pulled my refugee outfit out of my rucksack: some smart black trousers, an elegant shirt, shoes and socks. My father had given me a full uniform to don if I found myself in a city or near a residential area.

My smuggler from Bielefeld had also impressed upon me in Rome that I had to blend in. 'You don't stick out that way! A policeman's eye scans your clothes first. If something catches his gaze, then it moves to your skin and hair colour next. Fancy clothes are as important as ID in the West. The more elegant and stylish you look, the safer you'll be.'

So I stood under a tree in the middle of the countryside and changed my outfit. For a second I saw myself from the outside, cowering in my underpants in the snow without a clue where on the planet I was. I suddenly felt completely alone under that fine-looking tree—more alone than I'd ever felt before.

Despite all my fears, the journey had gone smoothly thus far, but I didn't really trust the peace and quiet. My mood turned as dark as the sky in this alien country. That might also have been due to the unspeakable cold, which clawed me like a rabid beast and set me shivering and shaking.

Of my old clothes I kept only the black jacket and the belt, abandoning the rest there on the ground. I made my way to the station in my fresh clothes. I trudged along the road through the slush and when I reached the first houses, I took a couple of detours and tried to stay off the main road as much as possible.

After half an hour's walk, I came to a building. A train was passing behind it. This had to be the station. I was about to go inside to find out where I was before ringing Murad in Paris to ask him for advice on how to proceed. Yet I had barely set foot inside the station when two men in beige trousers and green jackets, ignoring my transformation into a dapper gentleman, stepped forward and said, 'Police! Your papers, please!'

'What?'

'Passport?'

'No.'

A few moments later, the handcuffs clicked into place and I was led away to the police station a matter of yards from the railway station.

'I am from Iraq. Seeking asylum. Asylum, please.'

I had practised these words in advance in the quiet of my mind, day after day, but now, finally, I spoke them. I had better not say anything else, other than my name, my profession and my age. The smugglers had hammered home to us that we should only say more in the presence of an interpreter or civilians.

I was taken to an office where there were two men in uniform sitting side by side at a table. They talked to me. One of them copied the information from my papers into a notebook. He wanted to take down the names of the places I'd passed through on my way to Germany, but I didn't answer. I gave my profession as 'student'.

The man also asked if I was carrying any money on me. I said no, although this was untrue because my mother had sewn a few dollars into my clothes. Before I left home in Baghdad, she had opened the waistband, stuffed five hundred dollars inside and then sewn it back up again so that 'nobody, not even the devil himself, would guess that there's something hidden in here. Take them out only when you've reached your destination,' she said, wiping a tear from her cheek. 'It's your seed capital abroad.'

I was led into an adjacent room furnished with a table and several chairs. All the walls were bare. After a few minutes, the two police officers who had arrested me appeared again. They were wearing rubber gloves and told me to take off all my clothes.

'What?'

'Come on! Take your clothes off!'

'No!'

'Undress! Hurry up!'

Reluctantly I undressed while the two of them watched. I could see in their eyes how my torso both sickened and fascinated them. Yes, *Frau* Schulz, they saw something I'm deeply ashamed of to this day. They saw the real reason I had fled. I've been trying for years to keep it hidden from everyone. I may tell you about it later.

The unshaven policeman pointed to my underpants.

'Those too!'

'No!'

'Take them off!' he ordered, advancing menacingly towards me and glaring straight at me.

I obeyed and pushed down my pants.

The unshaven policeman began to search me. Every last nook and cranny, including my nuts. For the first time in my life someone stuck his finger in my arse.

Meanwhile, the other policeman checked my clothes and the rucksack. He sliced open the waistband, as if he did it a thousand times per day. He found the five hundred dollars and stacked them on the table. He pulled my birth certificate, my identity card, my high-school diploma and the four packets of Marlboros out of my bag and laid them next to the money.

'Put your clothes on, but not the belt! Understand?'

One of the policemen noted something on a form, pushed the sheet towards me and handed me a pen. 'Signature!' He tapped again and again with his index finger on the spot where I was presumably supposed to write my name. He did this in such a manner that I decided not to say 'No' again.

The two of them then led me into a new room, where I had my photo and my fingerprints taken.

After that, the nut-groper escorted me along the corridor and down some stairs into the basement. We came to a thick, heavy door. He opened it to reveal a second door right behind it, though this one was fitted with a wheel. He activated the mechanism and heaved the thick steel door open with some difficulty. A few paces further on, we came to another steel door, which the police officer also opened. I mustered all my courage and addressed him.

'Excuse me. Where am I? France? Paris? Where?'

The policeman looked at me as if I were completely mad. 'Are you kidding me? You are in Germany. Dachau. Understand?'

'Dachau? What's that?'

I'm delighted now that I'd never heard of Dachau before arriving in Germany. Had I known about the former Nazi concentration camp, my heart would definitely have stopped beating that day. Even so, my prison cell in Dachau still felt very sinister. The room reminded me of a milk bottle. Everything in it was white: the walls, the bed sheets, the washbasin and the toilet, the toilet roll, the radiator and also the table and chair, which were both screwed to the wall and the floor, as if they were untamed dogs that had to be kept on a leash. Or as if someone might steal them. The only thing of a different colour was above the bed: a red button. I was to ring it if I needed anything, the policeman explained before leaving the room and locking me inside.

I cowered in that cell for an age. After a while I could no longer tell if it was day or night, as the steady, cold light from a white halogen lamp destroyed all sense of time. I heard no voices, no cars and no trains, even though the police station was right next to the railway. Not even the tiniest sound reached my ears. Not a single smell. Nothing apart from the strange fug of the cell, the stench of loneliness. Colossal silence. Countless questions and fears whizzed through my brain, vertically, horizontally, diagonally and in weird circles. The seconds, minutes and hours crawled sluggishly past. I threw up three times into the toilet bowl despite not having eaten anything for days. It was as if my stomach were trying to break out of my body with my soul. My head hurt. I began to shiver, even though it wasn't cold. I scratched behind my ears and chewed my lip obsessively. The thought of a cigarette began to take total control of me. I stared at the red button for an eternity before finally pressing it. It was a few minutes before a policeman came and opened the door.

'What?'

'I need to eat, please. And a cigarette?'

'It's the middle of the night. Ask tomorrow.' He went away again, locking the various doors.

Fuckface! I grumbled to myself.

I lay down again, studied the white ceiling overhead and turned onto my left side so that the pristine white wall was directly in front of my nose.

I would have gladly discovered some cracks or a damp blotch there that would allow me to interpret or imagine something. Moist stones can conjure up shapes and even whole paintings in the brain, but the monotonous walls of Dachau spelt nothing but uncertainty and desolation.

I did actually doze off, although terrible nightmares soon tore me from my sleep again. I banged on the red button and waited. Nobody came. I got up, washed my face, drank from the tap and looked around in vain for a switch to turn out the light. I sat down on the floor and wrapped my arms tightly around my torso before getting back onto the bed. I pulled the sheet over my head.

'Yes, what do you want?' Suddenly there was a red-haired girl standing in my cell. She had the same uniform as the policemen. I stared at her in surprise.

'What do you want?'

'I'm hungry. No food for a thousand days!'

'I'll bring you something.'

I pulled the sheet back over my head to wait, and eventually the girl reappeared with two cheese rolls.

'It looks like you have been forgotten by my colleagues. I apologize for that.' She put the plate with the two rolls down on the table and made to leave straight away.

'May I ask you what time it is?'

'It's six in the morning.'

The door clicked shut. I fell upon the first cheese roll. Within a few bites I felt so sick that I had to force myself to eat more slowly so I wouldn't throw up again. I tore the roll into small pieces, sucked on the dough and chewed the cheese as slowly as possible. When I'd eaten both rolls and drunk a few mouthfuls of water, I felt some life returning to me. I fell asleep and only woke up again when the door was flung open once more. A policeman stepped into the room. He ordered me to stand up. As I was trying to ask him what was going to happen next, he grabbed me, pulled me from the bed, put handcuffs on me and dragged me out into the corridor. He shoved me along in front of him. We climbed the stairs and entered the same office where his colleagues had taken down my personal details.

It was fairly light outside, presumably morning. One of the three police officers present exchanged a few words with my bad-tempered guard. After I had signed a slip of paper, he accompanied me outside.

It was odd to see daylight again, and it dazzled me. A cold wind struck my face, too. Grey skies over Dachau. Virtually the entire car park, where a few patrol cars stood, was covered with snow. I was led to a car in which another police officer was waiting for us. I was put in the back, and then the three of us drove off.

I'd have liked to take in my surroundings, but I wasn't able to concentrate. I was extremely intimidated by the harshness and the cold and kept my eyes on the deadly serious men in front of me, trying to figure out what they had in mind. Where were they taking me?

After a long time, we drove up to a building that looked like a jail. My pulse began to race, and although I was sitting down, my legs were trembling. I could in fact make out the bars on the windows, but I also spotted people freely crossing the compound or walking away from it. No guards. Lots of black-haired people everywhere. I thought I identified a fellow countryman by his appearance. He was fiddling with prayer beads, just like old men did back home.

We pulled up in front of a smaller building and got out. They unlocked my handcuffs. I was given back my rucksack and taken to a room. I waited there for a short while, then two men in civilian clothes entered. The light-skinned one said, 'Hello', and the black-haired one greeted me in Arabic, saying, 'As-salamu alaikum.'

It was so wonderful to hear my mother tongue again. At last someone I can talk to, I thought. He looked friendly and was well dressed and clean-shaven.

The police officers left, and my new companions led me to another waiting room before disappearing again. There were already three men and two women sitting there in silence. After much musing, I checked my rucksack. Almost everything was still there including my belt, but not the five hundred dollars. The four packs of Marlboros were also gone. What a bunch of arseholes.

Suddenly the black-haired man was standing in front of me. 'Everything okay?'

'Yes, thanks. Where am I? And what is this place?'

'You're in Munich, and this is a hostel for asylum seekers.'

'What's going to happen to me?'

'They'll take down your details and give you some papers. Don't worry, it won't take long! Then you'll be taken to a place called Zirndorf where there's a hostel. There are no places free here in Munich: everywhere's full. The bus will be waiting outside at one o'clock.'

'I'm not going to prison, am I?'

'You have a right to asylum. You do have to pay a fine, though, because you're in the country illegally. That's why they confiscated the money you were carrying. Things would be easier for you now if you'd registered with the police.'

'Can I make a phone call? I don't want to stay here. I've got to travel on to Paris.'

'Please don't do anything stupid! Your fingerprints have been taken and sent to other European countries. You can't apply for asylum anywhere other than Germany because you were picked up here. This is your journey's end, your final stop in Europe. You'll have to get used to that idea!'

The man said goodbye and went back into the next room. On his way out, he stopped for a second in the doorway, turned to me again and gave me a friendly smile. 'Zirndorf is your Paris now. You can call from there.'

Throughout my escape from Iraq I kept finding myself in vehicles that took me to completely unfamiliar places whose names I found impossible even to pronounce. Now my journey was supposedly coming to an end, and the name of my future place of residence sounds like a little-known brand of medicine: Zirndorf.

The bus driver was standing outside the fence, casting bored glances at the building on the inside. He was chain-smoking and constantly spitting on the ground, as if he were bent on cursing the earth. When we finally set off, he devoted his entire attention to the other vehicles on the street and the myriad of signs. He steered the bus through Munich's dense traffic with consummate skill, seemingly indifferent to his passengers. His slim companion, on the other hand, tried to make the trip as pleasant as possible for us. Matthias—for that was how he had introduced himself—worked for a foundation that looked after asylum applicants. His hand gestures brought to mind a pianist's or a ballet dancer's. He flicked through a file, reading out a name from time to time. He studied each of us politely with somewhat dreamy eyes.

'You can tell he's queer from the way he looks at us!' said one of the lads in the back row.

'You fancy him or something?' someone called out, and everyone cracked up laughing.

'Oh, be quiet! He's nice to us. He doesn't deserve to be talked about like that. Have some respect! Maybe he can even understand Arabic!' said the boy next to me, whose name Matthias had just announced as Hassan.

'He can speak Persian and Hindi too! He's an Abbasidian caliph's eunuch who's taken a time machine here from the Middle Ages, straight from the palace in Baghdad. You numbskull!'

'I wish I didn't understand Arabic with all the rubbish you're spouting!'

'Oh, so you think you're something special, do you? Watch out or I'll come over there and punch you so hard your teeth'll scatter like coins!'

'Give me your best shot!' shouted Hassan, leaping at the other boy, his chest all puffed out. Roars of encouragement immediately transformed the bus into a cockfighting pit. Two older men stepped between the two of them, trying to stop their argument from escalating into a fistfight. Even the oldest man on the bus eventually got involved. He must have been over seventy, had a black turban wrapped around his head and was sitting right at the front behind the driver. His body was completely shrouded in a long brown robe. He looked like one of the tribal chiefs I had only ever seen on TV, and his voice was deep and imposing.

'Do you want to make us look ridiculous in the eyes of this country's people? I don't want to hear another sound from you. Do you understand? Show some respect, you ill-mannered scoundrels!'

His words brought the dispute to an abrupt end. No one said anything. Typical, I thought; our elders always have the last word, even in Europe.

I imagined that this bus with all of us inside had landed in Germany completely by accident. A few moments ago it had been driving through Baghdad as usual before it smashed into a wall and all of sudden, as in a fantasy film, it was caught up in a thick cloud of dust. A second later, it was speeding along a German motorway, but the hands of its passengers' watches were stuck on Mesopotamian time.

I kept glancing through the window at the absurd world outside known as Bavaria. After Munich's houses and shops and creatures wearing many clothes, caps, gloves and heavy coats, all that lay before us now was snowbound countryside. There were glimpses of the odd village in the distance. Occasionally a factory, a petrol station, a Burger King or a DIY store would appear.

Having calmed down now, Hassan told me that although we were on our way to Zirndorf, we wouldn't be staying there for very long. It was a stopover point, from where asylum seekers would be dispatched to a variety of different places. That's all he said and he didn't ask what my name was. Instead, he stared silently out of the window at the isolated villages we were speeding past.

The bus slowed to a stop outside a tiny house on a hilltop in the middle of some woods. Matthias asked a boy to get off. He escorted him into the house, came back alone and we drove on.

'Is that our fate too? To be dropped off on a hill in the woods?' asked Hassan. We'd been driving for a few more minutes when he suddenly started to feel sick. He immediately called for Matthias and explained his dire state, but Hassan puked in the middle of the aisle before the driver could stop the bus. He looked up, yellow bile dripping from his mouth. 'I only wanted to show what I think of our present situation.' He laughed, and a few men joined in, but others looked away, shaking their heads with disgust. Hassan was laughing, but I noticed tears welling up in his deep black eyes.

After a short break for Matthias and Hassan to wipe up the sick, we drove on. I fell asleep, waking only to find that it was dusk and we'd arrived. Our bus had pulled up outside Zirndorf asylum seekers' hostel.

There were no tarmacked roads here, only gravel tracks as thin as the firs on the surrounding hills. Like the place where we'd dropped the boy off, this one was on a hill, but it was much bigger. There were several main buildings and outbuildings.

We queued outside an office in the courtyard. A grey-haired man called out our names. An old woman, who had taken up a position beside him, handed each of us a bottle of apple juice, two bread rolls, four slices of cheese and a blanket. Next, the grey-haired man led us into a room that had presumably once been a gymnasium, a warehouse or a garage, but now there were lots of mattresses on the floor. This was where we would spend the night.

Although there were more than seventy men in that hall, at some stage all conversation, swearing and even rare bursts of laughter died away, the silence broken only by snoring and the odd lusty fart.

I sat bolt upright on my mattress. I tried to catch a glimpse of our surroundings through the large window on the side wall. It was pitch-black, and no stars, moon, aeroplane lights or shooting stars were to be seen in the sky. The window was rectangular, and the black surface looked like one of the censor bars I knew from TV. I knew that this new country I was now forced to call home had a face—but I couldn't yet tell if it was friendly or nasty.

Eventually I lay down, still brooding. My mattress was pressed up against the wall, so I was able to inspect it closely and make out the outline of some scribbling through the fresh paint. I recognized some Arabic lettering but couldn't decipher any words, let alone whole sentences. Only the word 'Allah' leapt out at me, and it cut me to the quick, for no matter how godforsaken I felt at that precise moment, he was the last person I could rely on for help. With a silent curse on my lips, I fell asleep.

The next thing I knew I heard a voice calling my name. I was immediately wide awake and jumped to my feet. It was already early morning. I had to go straight to the office to sign some documents. Next, I went to see someone from the charity Caritas. We spoke in English. I asked her about my money. She too said that the five hundred dollars must have been kept as a fine due to my illegal entry onto German territory. She had no explanation for the four missing packets of Marlboros either. They had probably simply gone up in smoke into the Dachau policemen's lungs.

I was given a ticket and a timetable in English along with five deutschmarks as pocket money. I was now supposed to continue my journey alone to a new hostel by bus and train. My next destination sounded like the Lebanese capital.

'To Beirut?' I asked the taciturn official who walked me to the bus stop.

'Yes, Bayreuth. It isn't far.'

So I took the bus to Zirndorf station. There, I found a phone booth and used my pocket money to call Murad in Paris at long last.

'Hi, Uncle Murad. It's me, Karim!'

'Oh my God. Karim! We've been so worried about you. Are you okay? Where are you?' Uncle Murad was beside himself with joy.

'Everything's fine. I'm in Germany.'

'What?'

'I've no idea how it happened. The smuggler dropped me off somewhere here, and I've spent the past few days in jail. Now I'm free again and I'm supposed to go to a hostel for asylum seekers. What should I do?'

'Did they take your fingerprints?'

'Yes, of course.'

'That's disgraceful! You'll have to forget about Paris and try to get asylum in Germany. There's nothing else you can do for the moment.'

'But this is a total balls-up, Uncle Murad. This wasn't how it was meant to be.'

'I'll take care of that damn trafficker.'

'Can you ring Dad and let him know I've made it?'

'Sure. Take care of yourself, lad, and call me if you need anything.'

Murad hung up. I held the receiver to my ear for a little longer, listening to the disconnect tone, unable to move. That endless, steady beeping sounded like the medical signal that a patient had died.

In Bayreuth I lived in a room measuring 215 square feet with three other Iraqis—Ali, Salim and Rafid. Our room was on the first floor, and when we looked out of our window we could see the yard and the opposite house, which accommodated families.

The hostel in Bayreuth, dear *Frau* Schulz, is a spacious compound made up of several buildings. The compound is set up for asylum seekers: it has a representative of the Federal Office for Migration and Refugees, a police bureau, a Caritas office and, obviously, accommodation for asylum seekers. It is on the edge of town and apparently used to be an army barracks, but it might have been a prison or a plague house.

Every building has exactly the same layout. Next to the entrance on the ground floor is a small room like a kiosk. An armed guard sits inside it, sizing up the passers-by and checking their identity cards, rucksacks and shopping bags. In front of him lie all kinds of half-eaten sweets, open packs of cigarettes and magazines, which keep him occupied when he isn't tormenting us with inspections. Each house has three floors, and at the near end of every corridor there are shared toilets, a bathroom and a kitchen. After those come the rooms.

The various parts of the hostel were named after the nationality of their occupants when I was there. There was the 'Albanian Area', the 'African Corner', the 'Afghan Space' and the 'Belarusian Room'. On the first floor a few Albanians and four Nepalese lived in two of the rooms, but the rest belonged to us Iraqis, so the whole floor was known as the 'Mesopotamian Corridor'. The Kurds had their own floor too, and the Christians were housed in the 'Christian Block' on the third floor. The remaining residents lived on the ground floor—Kirghiz, Pakistanis, Iranians, Montenegrins and Kazakhs. That section was known as the 'Orient Express'.

New arrivals obviously want to be housed with their fellow countrymen, and Caritas did in fact make sure that officials sent them where they'd fit in. Luckily, therefore, I was put with the Arab residents on the Mesopotamian Corridor.

There were only three women on our floor—one from Albania and two Nepalese. The latter had travelled from home with their lovers, whereas the gorgeous Albanian girl had come with her strapping brother. None of us ever entertained the slightest intention of flirting with her. Her brother's massive muscles bulged like the Great Wall of China in front of any bloke who so much as dreamt of talking to her. Yet a few brave souls would always hang out in the communal kitchen whenever the Albanian girl was cooking and her brother happened to be absent for a few seconds. They would all attempt to impress the Albanian girl with their culinary tips, each acting like the greatest chef in the history of mankind. She stoically put up with their palaver, assuming an impregnable smile, listening to them attentively and not answering as a rule. She would then saunter back to her room carrying the meal she had cooked. She must have guessed that every single one of her gazelle-like steps, every swish of her elegant backside, broke someone's heart every time.

The Iraqi and other Arab families lived in a house that was closer to the main road than ours. There were even a few single young women among them. Unfortunately, young men like us were banned from entering the building—not by the guards, but by our own Arab laws.

The hostel was overwhelmingly populated by unmarried men or men who had travelled without their families. The centre was our home, and we were not allowed to venture beyond a twenty-mile radius. The invisible fence holding us captive was called 'mandatory residence'.

It was mid-January, and it snowed day and night. I remember—it must have been about six in the morning on my first or second night there—how my bladder was so full that I struggled out of bed after my wake-up cigarette and shuffled along the corridor to the toilet. The entire hostel was deathly silent at that time of the morning. It was amazing because noiselessness was not otherwise natural to that place. During the day one could hear laughter, shouting, insults, cursing, arguments and conversations on all sides. The residents were like a troop of caged monkeys, never resting and producing a constant stream of noise.

As I went out into the corridor, the full force of that mean European chill hit me. It assailed me like a monster and bit through my skin to the bone. My hefty buttocks quivered like a samba dancer. I groped for the light switch and, teeth chattering, darted along the corridor which seemed to stretch out before me like a football pitch.

The toilets looked terrible. The floor was wet and grimy. I went into one of the stalls. The once-white plastic seat was yellow from urine, age and crushed cigarettes. What the hell, I really don't have a choice, I thought, pulling down my pyjama bottoms.

My penis had disappeared. Seriously. It had withdrawn far into my body. I panicked. I'd never experienced anything like this before. What kind of weird country is this where the weather's so shit? I had some trouble teasing my dick out from under my skin so that I could even pee. Touching my penis with my ice-cold hands was equivalent to administering an electric shock to myself. I felt as if I were holding a tiny nipple between my fingertips, although I'm pretty well hung at normal temperatures.

Eventually I couldn't resist the urge to dangle at least one finger under the jet to warm myself up a little. My urine was steaming like a geyser. When I'd finished I pulled up my bottoms. I noticed a few droplets of urine seeping through my underpants. The cold must have hurried me so much that I hadn't shaken myself off properly. There were no towels and no water heater in the bathroom, so I washed my hands only when I got back to our room. We had a strange contraption above our washbasin, which stored a very small quantity of water but heated it to a temperature that also allowed us to make tea. That morning I completely drained the reservoir to warm my hands, burrowed my way back under the covers and swore by all that was holy that never again would I get out of bed so early in the morning in this strange country where the weather was capable of making your genitals vanish.

I'd never experienced weather quite like it before. It never stopped snowing. The flakes tumbled from the sky, covering absolutely everything, even the tip of a church spire that was visible from the hostel. On my walks I also saw snow lashing terraces and windows decorated with fairy lights and eerie dwarves, beating down on pedestrians' hats and caps and slapping the earnest locals in the face. Snowflakes collected in every nook and cranny. Like a sandstorm they coated the ground, walls and trees with a new skin, making everything even greyer, like a pasty white corpse.

For days I studied the snowbound world outside my window. I got the impression that everything around me had been painted white: the yard, the vehicles in the car park, the main road, the black coats of the guard and the Caritas worker, who would go outside from time to time for a smoke. It was minus sixteen. That's sick. In Baghdad, *Frau* Schulz, such weather would be interpreted as an unequivocal sign of imminent apocalypse.

I was also puzzled by how you were supposed to walk in the snow. I felt as if I were wading through a swamp, as my feet kept getting sucked down into squelching sinkholes. Never before had I worn so many clothes on top of each other. I felt as if I'd put on forty pounds. All those layers made it hard to walk and it took a long time for me to adjust to this. I looked unbelievably silly. I'd assembled my winter outfit from donated clothes: a brown lumberjack's shirt, a thick, light-blue down jacket, mittens emblazoned with characters from the film *The Lion King*, a yellow scarf, a black woollen beanie with a Chicago Bulls logo on it, white-and-blue batik jeans and two pairs of white sports socks over a further pair of thin black women's socks and a pair of grey long johns.

All of these clothes had been provided by a nice old woman from Caritas called Karin Schmitt. Shortly after I arrived, she saw me running across the courtyard in my summer clothes and came striding furiously towards me with an interpreter.

'Are you out of your mind? This isn't the Sahara, you know. You'll die like that. My God, just look at you!'

I wondered quite what she imagined. First, I had never owned any winter clothes and, second, it would have been impossible for me to escape lugging a large suitcase filled with functional clothing for every conceivable adventure.

'Last winter a refugee lost two toes to the cold! His smuggler abandoned him somewhere in the Bavarian Forest, and the poor guy had nothing but summer clothing on. They found him lying on a main road. The doctors confirmed that he was suffering from third-degree frostbite to his hands and feet. They said he'd almost died. So please don't be an idiot and put on some warm clothes!'

Without Karin I would probably have lost a toe or two of my own. She and I selected a few items of clothing, although from a fashion point of view the choice was limited. Rafid was the first to erupt into gales of laughter when my roommates caught sight of me in my bizarre polar explorer's get-up.

'Oh, you look shit! Like a multi-coloured onion!'

In spite of all my protective gear I was so cold every time I went outside that I would rather have turned around and crawled straight back into my room to hibernate there like a bat. The others would often drag me out for walks against my will anyway.

'Don't be such a wimp!' they shouted, grabbing me under both arms and dragging me over the threshold and out into the snow.

On the rare occasions I was out on my own, the town's many shops were part of my strategy for avoiding the unfamiliar cold. I would run into a different store every twenty yards, using it as a staging post. For example, I would store up a little warmth in Starbucks, then dash across the street to take refuge in Burger King or H&M. It got easier in the pedestrian zone because the shops were all in a line there.

This staging-post strategy was the only way I could cover longer distances across town in such low temperatures. The best place for any refugee in the whole of Bayreuth was without a doubt the Rotmain Centre. That wonderfully welcoming blast of hot air when you entered the two-storey shopping mall! It was warm everywhere, and you could people-watch without anyone bothering you. We stood around on our own or in small groups, observing people shopping or eating cake in the cafe. Strolling around Rotmain was the ideal way to kill time, since we were not allowed to learn German or work or do anything meaningful with our days. At the same time, this shopping centre lulled us into dreams of an ordinary life. How we'd have loved to be like them, shopping, sitting in a cafe, ordering drinks and chatting with one of the many young waitresses. But how was that ever going to happen? It was all around us and yet we were so very far away from it all. The locals went shopping, and we absorbed the warmth of their lives.

At the very beginning of my stay in the hostel, I had to go to the administrative office for questioning. I received a so-called identity card. This was a document confirming that I had a three-month residence permit. It was a green, oblong document bearing my photo and personal details. The official handed me another slip of paper as well.

'This is your appointment. On 21 February at 8.30 a.m. Please make sure you're on time! The state must check if you qualify for asylum, if you are a refugee as defined by the Geneva Refugee Convention or if there are any other obstacles to deportation. Understand? Well, bye for now.'

I left the office and walked back quickly across the courtyard to our house. It was still early morning. My roommates had just made some scrambled eggs and tea and they invited me to have breakfast with them. I'd just sat down on the floor and was loading some egg onto my toast with my fingers when Salim asked me about my grounds for claiming asylum.

'Desertion,' I said, keeping it short; I didn't want to tell him the whole story. However, that one word was more than enough information for him and the others.

'If you want to spend the rest of your life stuck in an asylum seekers' hostel,' said Rafid, 'then go ahead and tell them that.' He seemed very bitter all of a sudden, as if thinking about reasons for claiming asylum had spoilt his appetite. 'I'll tell you something: you have to come up with a completely new life story.' He stopped eating and rolled himself a cigarette.

I left my scrambled egg on toast where it was, drained my tea at once and, without asking, took a cigarette paper and some tobacco from his pouch. 'Meaning what?'

He lit my cigarette for me. 'Desertion isn't a good enough reason to request sanctuary here. If it were, anyone who'd ever tried to get out of military service or gone AWOL would be granted asylum. That's completely wishful thinking when you consider how many war zones and standing armies there are around the globe. You'll never get a residence permit if they find out you're here because you deserted. You'll get a temporary stay of deportation. That status does allow you to live outside the hostel, but you'll be tied to Bayreuth and you won't be allowed to travel, study or work. If you don't want a residence permit, then be truthful. I've been here for two months and I still have no idea if I can stay or if I'm going to be deported. It's not impossible that I made the biggest mistake of my life when I told the judge the truth. Actually, I didn't even tell him the whole truth, only a tiny part of it, and yet I deeply regret it.'

'A real judge?'

'A half-judge. My interpreter told me that civil servants are the ones who decide at the Ministry for Migration and Refugees. They decide if we should be allowed to stay or be deported. I've no idea what their real title is, and to be honest, I couldn't give a damn if they're called judges, executioners or something else entirely!'

I gazed into Rafid's dark, deep-set eyes. His features were tense. 'What do you think I should do when I stand in front of one of those judges?'

'You need instructions in this country. Everything's so laborious and complicated. Even buying a train ticket is a massive drama. There are hundreds and hundreds of different tickets. The Germans themselves don't always understand.'

'You're such a misery guts,' said Ali, putting his hand on Rafid's shoulder and giving him a good-natured tug. 'Stop it, will you? Don't be so ungrateful. You come to this country and all you do is complain about the people who've put a roof over your head.'

'Call this a "roof"? This is a jail—can't you get that into your thick skull? We are in an ice-cold, twelve-square-mile prison called Bayreuth.'

'Oh, stop!'

'Leave me alone!' Rafid swatted Ali's hands from his shoulders. The atmosphere in the room had suddenly become tense, and no one said anything for a moment. Then Rafid asked me, 'Tell me, Karim, how did you get here? By plane, train, car or on foot?'

'Various cars, a dinghy and a ship.'

'Well, nobody is ever to hear about that, okay? You came here by lorry. And you didn't set foot in any other European country on the way. That's the only way you'll have a right to asylum. Never, ever say that you were in another Western country, do you hear?'

'Yeah, yeah. We all know that.'

'The best thing is to tell them you escaped from Iraq with the help of a smuggler, for example via Turkey. There, he hid you in a lorry and brought you to Germany. Say that during the entire journey you saw only the inside of that truck and had no idea where you were. Nothing more.'

'But who's going to believe that kind of crap? How am I supposed to have survived for days on end in the back of a lorry? Where did I piss and shit? And you have to stretch your legs from time to time too.'

'Just tell them you used bottles and bags, and did squats.'

'That's not credible at all!'

'If you tell them you were in Rome, then they'll send you straight back to Italy because it's an asylum country. The Italians will immediately send you back to Germany in a police car. You'll probably get caught in a vicious circle for weeks or even months, tossed back and forth between the Italian and German border police like a ball.' He broke off for a second and shot me a cautionary look. 'What did you say to the police when you registered? Or did they catch you?'

'I was arrested.'

'Oh, that isn't a problem.'

'I didn't tell them anything. They took my fingerprints, photographed me, took down my personal details and then forgot me in their cell.'

'Then you can prepare yourself properly. I'm here if you need any help.'

'Of course I need help. What should I say to the judge? Why am I here now?'

'The basic rule is never to tell the truth! Say that you worked with the opposition, the state has been hunting you for years and you can't live there any more because you'll be thrown in jail and tortured or even executed. They've no way of checking that. It's not as if Saddam keeps a file on everyone and sends a copy to every asylum country. The main thing is to convince the judge of two things: first, that you can't go back to your homeland, and second, that you haven't set foot in another asylum country before.'

'I never meet a genuine opponent of the regime back home. Everyone I know rants about the government, but none of them has ever really done anything about it. And now this hostel is suddenly teeming with revolutionaries, or what?'

'Of course not all of us are political activists. Most of us haven't got a clue about politics. We still come here and apply for asylum, though. We just want to live our lives in peace. It's totally absurd that you first have to be harshly persecuted and tortured to earn the right to asylum.'

'I, for example,' Salim interjected, 'wasn't fleeing from Saddam, but from my father. He was a dictator! A genuinely gigantic arsehole!'

We all laughed.

'So what did you tell the judge?' I asked him, hoping to hear something of use to me.

'Not that, of course: he'd have thought I was a pubescent youth. I made up an exciting story. I seriously thought about becoming a writer after my hearing. I'm a grand liar, and a good one. But I'm not the only one here of whom that could be said. I met a guy in the kitchen earlier, a Syrian. I could tell where he came from straight away by his accent. He claimed to be an Iraqi. Last week a Kurd, who spoke no Arabic at all, lied to my face that he was an Arab from the south. Recently, a Palestinian even asked me quite casually what sights there were to see in Baghdad. Do you think he was asking because he's planning his next summer holidays in Iraq? No chance—he's going to pretend to be Iraqi.'

'Everyone knows that right now you're more likely to get asylum if you're an Iraqi,' said Rafid, 'than if you come from a country with no dictator—

or at least no vicious dictator. What's funny is that the Iraqi population outside Iraq is getting bigger and bigger. That's just how it is. People from many countries have no right to asylum here, so they pretend to be Iraqis to get a residence permit. The odds are stacked against Kurds, for example. They try to pass themselves off as Arabs.'

'But they *are* Iraqis,' I said, because what Rafid was saying made no sense.

'For you they are. For you they're Iraqis, but they've governed themselves in northern Iraq since the 1991 Gulf War, with the support of the Americans. They aren't entitled to asylum in Germany because they don't live in a dictatorship any more.'

'Oh man, this is so complicated.'

'No, it isn't. I didn't have a clue at first either. In a week you'll be helping the newcomers like I'm helping you. There's nothing else to do in this country than get bored, go to the Rotmain Centre or H&M or find out about the laws and regulations and maybe identify some new loophole that ensures our survival.'

'Have you got any more useful tips so I'll be ready for my hearing?'

'Come up with details for your story! You have to learn the dates and names by heart. Same for places and times. The judge will ask you again for information you've already provided, just to see if you contradict yourself. You have to know it all off by heart! Repeat your story to yourself until you believe that everything really happened that way. Go through the lie in your head until you genuinely believe it's true!'

Acquiring at least a basic understanding of the many clauses and regulations under which this land is buried became my most pressing task, *Frau* Schulz. I had learnt to hate the Iraqi administrative apparatus early on because its chaotic and bureaucratic workings are like merciless divine retribution. Now, the mindless, soulless German authorities really pushed me over the edge. A few minutes of thinking about all the obstacles I had to negotiate left me exhausted, and I tried to patch together an account of my life that the law might acknowledge. During this period, I generally spent the whole day lying on my bed, feeling jaded and overwhelmed. Every minute I wished that the day of my hearing would finally be over—and that I might win this crazy lottery.

Three weeks passed, and I still hadn't come up with a suitable lie to persuade the judge to grant me asylum. All at once, my true past struck me as silly and trifling. I felt sick, although I'd always thought that my biography was actually quite exciting. Like most Iraqis, I had experienced enough tragic events to fill several lives. Yet German law suddenly made those experiences appear trivial because either they didn't tick the right boxes or I couldn't provide any evidence for them. All of a sudden I had no idea how to behave, and I even began to wonder why I'd run away from Iraq in the first place.

The stuff about being a deserter was already a white lie. I didn't want to talk about the true reason to anyone. It's a personal matter, and I don't want people raking it over in public. To this day I still haven't told a soul, neither in Iraq nor Germany, to any agency, any tribunal or any friend—to anyone apart from a few doctors and nurses. And you, *Frau* Schulz. I will now tell you.

Dear *Frau* Schulz, until I was fourteen I had everything a boy requires to become a real man: a strong, flat chest and a powerful voice. I strode barefoot and bare-chested across the main square in my neighbourhood of Baghdad. I strutted around from morning to evening, the sun shimmering on my brown skin.

Then I reached puberty. Physical changes quickly set in. My shoulders and ribcage broadened, my voice broke, my body hair grew and so, of course, did my interest in sex. Suddenly, naked women populated my dreams, having it off with me in every conceivable way and position. I often recognized my teachers, cousins, neighbours, school friends and then my sister Samira—something that ashamed me terribly even in my sleep. I would often wake up to find my underpants wet. My desire for sex was so overpowering that I would often hide under my covers during the day to masturbate. Once I even wanked in the school toilets with four classmates over a photo of a blonde nude model. Yet even as other lads and I scoured market after market in Baghdad for new naked photos, the most traumatic experience of my life began.

Standing under the shower in our bathroom, I clutched my penis in my right hand while stroking my upper body with my left. I was startled because it suddenly seemed completely different. It felt as if my chest had swollen. At first I thought that all the masturbating might have inflated my chest muscles, and thought no more of it. Over the following days, however, my body went into complete overdrive. Within a very short space of time I grew breasts—real breasts.

Every day I touched them and noticed that they were becoming rounder and fuller. After only a few weeks, I had a genuine bosom instead of my hard manly chest.

I was in shock. I kept running into the bathroom and would stand there in front of the mirror, staring at this boy with boobs with a mixture of revulsion and fear. I felt as if it was no longer my own body, and that I was metamorphosing into a monster. I wouldn't have been surprised if my penis had turned into a vagina. I barely dared to masturbate any more: the changes in my body had robbed me of any desire to do so. I would touch my penis every few days, purely to reassure myself that it was still there.

I also began to picture my backside expanding until it was as round as Samira's. Here, at least, all it took was a few hearty pinches to tell me that my bottom was as firm and muscular as ever. Nevertheless, I got the insidious feeling that a female spirit was lurking inside me—at least in the upper half of my body, whereas the lower half remained that of a man.

At night I dreamt of things that sent fear flooding through my veins. Men kissed and bit my breasts. One by one they clambered on top of me and raped me. I wept bitterly and begged them to stop. One of them slobbered as he shouted 'Shut up!' and hit me in the face. I screamed and woke up bathed in sweat. I took a quick glance in the mirror beside my bed, but in it I saw not my own face but my girlfriend Hayat's.

Have a little patience, *Frau* Schulz. At this point I have to take a short break and roll myself a joint. I find it hard to talk about Hayat. She's the reason I can't cope with quite a lot of things in life. For example, it's because of her that I avoid the ubiquitous Turkish supermarkets here, and it's due to Hayat that Jehovah's Witnesses make me nervous.

I've only entered a Turkish supermarket once since I arrived in Germany. I broke out in a sweat and swore that I'd never go in one again. Ever since, I have bought my stuff in normal supermarkets such as Lidl or Norma, although I find their range limited in comparison to the number of products the Turks have on offer. However, German supermarkets do not stock the brand of mineral water that always upsets me because the word HAYAT is emblazoned on every bottle in blue lettering. (By the way, the Turks appear to have adopted this Arabic word quite indiscriminately. It means 'life'. Those bloody Ottomans! They stole everything from their colonies, and even 'life' from our language.)

As for Jehovah's Witnesses, I sometimes felt like throwing them out of the window when they came calling yet again. Every month they would knock on my door at the hostel to proselytize and hand me their Arabic brochures. 'Life before Death', 'Life after Death' or simply 'Life'—Hayat, Hayat, Hayat.

For years I tried to ignore this word, using 'world', 'cosmos', 'universe' and 'here and now' depending on the context, but never 'Hayat'. The word 'life' is still a dagger plunged deep into my heart. The mere sound of it causes me almost unbearable pain.

The last time I saw my Hayat, *Frau* Schulz, I was twelve years old and didn't yet have my breast problem. Back then, my looks were any mother's dream: gleaming, pitch-black hair, piercing eyes as keen as a bird of prey's, and a sleek yet powerful physique. I was very popular with my female relatives, the ladies from our neighbourhood and my women teachers. They would regularly shower me with kisses and caresses. That's how I met my first girlfriend, Hayat, at the tender age of eight.

She was nearly eight hundred days older than me, which seemed to us like half a lifetime back then. Her beauty was such a mystery to me that I sometimes thought she must be a mermaid risen from the ocean depths. Her brown hair reminded me of the mane of a Spanish horse, the whites of her black eyes shone like the crescent moon on a summer's night and her tiny nose was like Maya the Bee's.

Everyone thought Hayat was by some distance the most attractive girl in the whole district, yet she had a different lot in life: she was deaf and mute. I could easily understand her, though, for she communicated with her hands and her eyes.

Although Hayat was as slim and delicate as a match, she was still known as 'the Tank' because she acted like one whenever she sensed danger. She once hurled a stone at a boy's head with all her might, and blood came gushing from his forehead like water from a tap. He had tried to grope her bottom. From that day on, the boy was known as 'Fountainhead' rather than by his real name.

People in our neighbourhood considered Hayat retarded due to her muteness and her behaviour. I, however, thought she was perfect—gentle *and* rebellious. She struck me as being like a young, green branch that looks immature and delicate, yet will neither burn nor break.

When Hayat turned thirteen, her body began to become more feminine. Her breasts were suddenly as round and mystical as the domes of a magnificent mosque. I became increasingly anxious that others might try to steal Hayat from me. It was impossible to ignore the local men ogling her backside, and it was impossible not to overhear them talking and whispering about her. I knew that every man wanted to marry a girl as beautiful as Hayat, even if she was deaf and dumb.

Yet the notion that someone else might marry her horrified me. Hayat would have barely ventured out into the street afterwards. She would have had to stay in her husband's house, and if she did come out, then only hidden behind a veil that would have concealed her wonderful hair from me.

One summer's day, *Frau* Schulz, I came home from school, ate with my family and then went outside as usual to get up to some mischief. The boys gathered in our local square to play football, fight or hunt sparrows with their catapults. A few girls joined us, while others played their own games or stood chatting in small groups. I waited outside the ice-cream shop for Hayat as every day, but that day she didn't come. At some point I decided I wasn't going to stand around for any longer, but would go and look for her instead. I walked to her parents' house and knocked on the door, but there was no answer. I peered cautiously through the keyhole and called, 'Hello?' No answer. The courtyard was deserted. Nothing there but rubbish. I walked around the left side of the house and tried to peek through the living-room window. Nothing. The house had been emptied: it looked as if nobody lived there any more.

An old woman suddenly appeared from nowhere. 'Go away, boy! You've got no business around here! Go away! Clear off!'

'I just want to see Hayat,' I said. 'Where is she?'

The old woman took off one of her shoes and waved it menacingly above her head. 'If you don't get out of here right now, my shoe is going to kiss your gob!'

I scarpered and, glancing back, saw the woman still standing outside the house like a sentry. I found out the following evening that Hayat's family had moved away. Where to? Nobody really knew. Why? Everybody knew that, *Frau* Schulz. Everybody but me.

I only heard a few days later. A girl from next door had seen Hayat getting into a car with three men. They apparently drove to the edge of our neighbourhood, where they raped her and left her corpse lying in the dust, like a bag of rubbish, right next to the children's cemetery.

I've tried countless times to recreate in my mind what she must have been through that day, how she suffered and the cruel manner in which she died. A recurring dream has haunted me ever since I learnt of Hayat's fate. In it Hayat is playing outside the school she's not allowed to attend because she's deaf and dumb. She comes here every day when she doesn't have to help her mother with the housework. She sits on a wall and watches the schoolchildren running around, screaming and pushing each other. Hayat is wearing a light dress with a pattern of white flowers on it, and she's holding a colourful book in her hands. She wants to be like the girl on the cover: *Alice in Wonderland.* I gave it to her for her thirteenth birthday. Hayat admires the maiden in the forest with the dazzling smile. 'I'm Alice,' she thinks, smiling at a sparrow that has alighted on the wall beside her.

She knows that she'll soon turn fourteen and can therefore expect a new present. She doesn't yet know that I plan to give her *Cinderella.* She'll probably leave her shoe lying around somewhere so that a handsome prince may find it and marry her.

She goes home and has lunch with her family, the same magical smile still on her lips, then comes over to my house. Together we walk to a spot in the city park where there's a small lake. She loves the butterflies there above all else. We play hide-and-seek and catch into the twilight hours. Reluctantly we make our way home. I give her a tender goodbye kiss on the cheek. We part and walk off in opposite directions.

Before Hayat reaches her family home, a large black car with tinted windows blocks her path. Three men get out, each holding an illustrated book. They show them to her. Hayat spots the beautiful girls on the covers and walks over to the strangers. She recognizes *Snow White*; the second man holds up *Sleeping Beauty* and the third, *Little Red Riding Hood.* She approaches. Yet every time she takes a step towards them, the men take a step backwards. Hayat seems mesmerized, snatching at the pictures. She walks towards the men whose faces are hidden behind the books. All of a sudden, one of them drops *Snow White* to reveal a fierce, bearded features, his eyes gazing lecherously at Hayat. He grabs her and pulls her violently towards him. Another man throws *Little Red Riding Hood* to the ground and knocks Hayat unconscious from behind. The three men drag her into the car, and the doors slam shut. The driver accelerates away. Hayat lies there. Everything around her is black, and beside her sleep Snow White, as white as snow, Sleeping Beauty, locked in her century-long slumber, and Little Red Riding Hood, her hood as red as blood.

I often wake from this dream sodden with sweat and trembling as if I'd truly witnessed what happened next. However, my unconscious refuses to show me the images that follow. I'm not sure whether their absence isn't in fact more excruciating.

Hayat's corpse was buried at the edge of our neighbourhood on the exact spot where the three men had raped and murdered her. Her parents didn't want their neighbours to find out what had happened. 'Lose your honour and you're dead, even if you're still breathing,' my mother said at the time as she wept. Hayat's parents packed their bags the day after the event, and even now nobody knows where they live.

One afternoon I asked my older sister Samira to go to Hayat's grave with me. We weren't usually allowed to venture into that part of town because my parents claimed it was dangerous. Murderers were continually discarding corpses there; the victims were virtually always women and children. It was actually an ordinary cemetery, though. The locals called it simply the 'children's cemetery', for there were mainly dead children buried there.

I was glad that Samira agreed to my wish and came along with me. We were scared stiff the whole way to the cemetery and didn't exchange a word. The area was barren and dusty, even the cemetery itself: nothing but yellow earth and the odd straggling weed. Here and there in the dirt lay a few stones with dead children's names daubed on them. We searched for Hayat's grave. I imagined that I was the prince who only had to kiss his Sleeping Beauty to release her from everlasting sleep. We looked for Hayat for nearly two hours, but we couldn't find her name anywhere. My head felt as heavy as lead. The many names of the dead wore me down, as did the thought that behind every series of letters there was a life, a person who had lived and been loved, a person like us. Then Samira thought she heard voices approaching.

'We'd better go. Maybe her family didn't want her name to become public and so they buried her anonymously.'

I looked around from time to time on our way back in the hope that I'd spot Hayat suddenly running after us. When we were almost home, the wind got up, and I felt something like a hand or a strand of hair gently stroking my cheek. Hayat—it was Hayat! I thought I could smell her. Shutting my eyes, I savoured this fleeting sense of closeness, which faded as quickly as it had appeared. When my sister noticed that I was crying, she bent down to me, embraced me and wept with me. I sobbed and sniffed, and all my bottled-up grief came pouring out. I wept uncontrollably for a long time.

Up to that point I had accepted Hayat's death with a strange lack of emotion and had been unable to mourn for her. Everything changed that day: in the preceding few hours I had said goodbye not only to Hayat but also to my childhood.

Sometimes, *Frau* Schulz, I think Hayat wanted to keep me company for the rest of my life, and that's why she donated part of her body to me from the hereafter. That's why I became such a weird creature, endowed with both a magnificent penis and an ample bosom. I conceal the latter to this day under the baggiest clothes I can find.

Back then in Baghdad I was also afraid that local lads would rape me if they ever discovered that I was half woman. I did my best to be a real tough guy, hung out with the men, tried to make my voice sound more forceful and gave powerful handshakes to one and all. My acting was pretty successful, but over time my breasts became larger and more visible when I jumped or ran or bent down. The solution was figure-hugging vests, which compressed my upper body.

At the time I was trying, through a great deal of sport, mainly press-ups, to create a firm manly chest and get rid of these unwanted breasts. I could feel the muscles under my breasts when I tensed them, but my bust remained as big as ever. I didn't know what the cause might be. I'd never heard of a man growing something like this—and I couldn't tell a soul.

Samira soon got married and moved out to live with her husband in a different part of Baghdad. I often visited her, sometimes spending the whole day at her house, but I still couldn't bring myself to tell her my problem. I hoped from the bottom of my heart each time we hugged, that she would notice and broach the subject of my breasts herself. All my hopes were in vain, though.

This physical turmoil completely changed my life. Swimming baths became a total no-go zone for me. I envied all the boys who could swan into the swimming baths half naked, just like that. I found it a relief that nobody else, with breasts or without, could swim in the lovely river Tigris that flows through Baghdad. That was because government officials, ministers and their families claimed the river for their own. They built luxury villas and palaces for themselves directly by the river, and the result was that almost everywhere was cordoned off and the only place you were allowed to swim in Baghdad was in a pool.

The next thing I was forced to give up was football. Despite wearing the tightest undershirt, the idea of having to get into my kit in a changing room with the other boys filled me with terror. I began to hate summer and instead loved Iraqi winters, which are pleasantly mild, unlike this icy misery here in Germany.

So I would largely withdraw in summer, spending most of my time at home. This in turn opened up a completely new world for me—the world of comics. I collected lots of magazines, supplements and even newspapers featuring cartoons. At the flea market, I could buy stories from many different Arab countries for a pittance, Saddam's censorship laws permitting. Soon I began to draw and invent stories myself, creating my own comic series about extraterrestrials who took over our world and were neither male nor female but something in-between. These aliens tried to eradicate male characteristics on our planet by cutting off men's genitals and implanting artificial vaginas in their place. I was the hero battling against them, of course.

I wanted a girlfriend, *Frau* Schulz. But how was I supposed to get one? I'm still plagued by a constant fear of men beating, humiliating or raping me, and of being mocked or considered disgusting by women.

I would probably never have thought of leaving my country if these horrible breasts hadn't appeared. However, life was carrying me relentlessly towards a huge problem—military service.

I often saw soldiers on TV, marching bare-chested across the parade ground shouting, 'Be prepared! Always prepared!' How would those soldiers look at me, were I to stand next to them, breasts jiggling, yelling, 'Be prepared! Always prepared!' How would those men, confined to barracks for months on end with no woman in sight, treat me?

Soldiers use a particular term when they consider someone unimportant: 'al-Arif', the sergeant's helper. This is a dogsbody who must take care of all kinds of chores for his superior: washing his clothes, cooking, carrying his bags and giving him a hand job at night if he so desires. These people are practically the generals' wives, often homosexual or turned into sex slaves. So rumour has it.

Back then I was prepared and determined to do whatever it took and go wherever necessary to avoid the army. I didn't want to be an al-Arif, and I even contemplated suicide. Yet it would ultimately depend on my high-school diploma whether I was to end up as a sex slave in a military barracks or as a student at university. It was the Ministry of Education that decided on the basis of a pupil's final grades if he went straight from school to the army or was allowed to go to university first. It was unclear where the cut-off point lay, however, because the criteria changed from one year to the next and they were never published. They were presumably determined by the government's need for soldiers at any given time.

I passed my final school exams with sixty-one out of a possible one hundred marks. Shortly afterwards, the ministry announced the minimum grade required to escape military service until after university: all school-leavers with lower grades were conscripted. That minimum grade was sixty-four.

I found the ensuing period incredibly tough. My suicidal thoughts became increasingly specific, but for my parents' sake I could never bring myself to go through with it. I was their sole remaining son. My older brother Halim had died in combat in 1991, and my mother had lost my younger brother in childbirth. It was this memory that deterred me from forcing my parents to cope with another loss. Although I didn't have the slightest confidence in the outcome, I decided to put an absurd proposal to my father.

'I'd like to study, Dad. I want to go abroad!'

'Yes, son. I don't want to lose you as well. I've been putting money aside for the past few years for precisely this eventuality. Go!'

I stared at him in disbelief. I thought he was joking. The longer he said nothing and we looked each other in the eye, the more obvious it became that he was serious. I threw my arms around him like a little boy. The very next day my father got in touch with his friend Murad in Paris and arranged a contact with people smugglers through some distant relatives.

I had repeatedly read and heard about surgeons in Europe who carried out very successful cosmetic operations. It was expensive but feasible, even for someone like me. I longed for nothing more than for a wonderfully flat manly chest. I wanted to feel a fully fledged man again after all this time; suicide didn't cross my mind any more. I harboured a growing desire to get a normal job abroad and save up so that one day I'd be able to afford the operation.

I did my best, *Frau* Schulz. I've been trying ever since I arrived in Germany, but working for the past three years hasn't brought in enough money, and my health insurance wasn't prepared to fund it, even though my general practitioner referred me to a psychiatrist, who confirmed after our conversation that my breasts were a psychological burden on me. That wasn't a sufficient reason for the insurance company to pay for such an expensive operation. The customer service centre justified its refusal by arguing that breasts were not a disease, after all. So earning enough money myself was the only option.

The doctor at the plastic surgery clinic here in Niederhofen diagnosed that I was suffering from what was known as gynaecomastia, due to a swelling of the breast glands. He said that it was actually a common phenomenon, which affected sixty per cent of all boys during puberty. There were various causes, he said, but in my case it was a disturbance of my hormonal balance. However, one intervention could drain off the fat, and that would be the end of my women's breasts. It might also be necessary to remove the superfluous skin and tighten it somewhat.

Doesn't that sound great, *Frau* Schulz? It sounds fantastic. But you know what doesn't sound so good? The surgery costs six thousand euros.

The doctor's quote hit me like a karate chop to the throat. I'd guessed it would be expensive, but that figure seemed totally astronomical. But still I went for it, right from the very start. For a year I worked like an animal, holding down several factory and cleaning jobs at once. Although my living expenses were low, terrible wages and tax deductions meant it was simply impossible for me to save up. My only hope was the German course, which I was finally allowed to start, so that I would be allowed to gain another high-school diploma and finally be able to study. I never got any further than the German lessons, though, and you know full well why, *Frau* Schulz. You sent me the revocation of my right to asylum, dashing at a stroke all my hopes. And I still have these breasts. Look at them.

Dear *Frau* Schulz, I left my homeland because I dreamt of becoming an ordinary man, that's all.

Standing over the toilet bowl, I unzip my fly while typing a text to Salim.

'How are you? When will you get here?'

I listen to the roar of the toilet flush, then go back into the living room and sit down on the sofa. The TV is still on mute. Paul Bremer, the US civilian administrator in Iraq, is blathering on in front of a large group of journalists. This is followed by last December's world-famous scene: Saddam being pulled out of his hidey-hole. He looks unwashed and unshaven, like a scruffy tramp. I pick up the remote and switch the sound back on. 'A wave of bomb attacks shakes Iraq,' says the ravishingly beautiful presenter in a headscarf. I turn the TV off.

I would love to ring my family, but I'd rather not tell anyone that today I will put myself in the hands of another smuggler. If I do, they're bound to worry about me. Maybe I should call my father when I get to Finland? Yes, that'd be more sensible.

My mobile vibrates. Admir's number appears on the display. Admir is my colleague at the building site, an Albanian. It was a big mistake to tell him I'll soon be leaving the country. Even though I didn't say why and where I was going, he hasn't left me alone since.

I've no idea what he wants from me. He keeps ringing me up to tell me his story. I've heard it umpteen times over the past week.

'This is my second time in Germany. The first time I only really came here for a woman. I'd got to know her in Tirana when she was on holiday. Anna and I met again in Munich. I was here illegally, staying with a fellow Albanian. Anna and I met again and again in the Englischer Garten. It was the best thing that had ever happened to me in my shitty life. We often sat there kissing, always on the same bench, and sometimes we even got it on in the bushes. Then, after two weeks, I proposed to her—and she answered that she had a boyfriend and didn't want to hang out with me any more. It was over, on the spot. I couldn't believe it. I was furious and very sad. The next evening I went back to the Englischer Garten, alone this time. I saw our bench and had the crazy idea of taking it with me. I wasn't bothered where I would take it; I just wanted to keep it as a reminder. I got hold of a shovel, stood by the bench again at midnight and began to dig it up. I almost managed, too. But before I could lift it and drag it away, two policemen came up and arrested me. It didn't take them long to deport me to Albania. Now I'm back, illegally again, working undeclared, saving a little, with only one goal in this country: I don't want to see Anna again; I just want to nick that bench and haul it back to Albania.'

I hang up on Admir and put my mobile on the table. I roll a cigarette and mix in a little hash.

Dear *Frau* Schulz, I was still in bed in the afternoon two days before my hearing; I hadn't got up all day.

'What's wrong with you?' asked Rafid. 'It's getting dark again, and you're still lying there! Aren't you well?'

'Damn, I want to go to Paris.'

Rafid didn't react to this. 'Fancy a beer later?'

'Are you nuts? We can't drink here. Ali's religious and he won't even stand the sight of alcohol. Anyway, I've got no money left.'

'We have an invitation. To the Christian Block. A new Iraqi Jesus-follower arrived yesterday. He sings and whistles well. It's bound to be a laugh.'

We drank our first beer at eight o'clock. Salim was there too. Even Ali joined us, although it was obvious that both the alcohol and the Christians made him uneasy.

'This tastes great. What is it?' I asked Zechariah, our host.

'Augustiner. From Bavaria.'

'Oh man!' Rafid interjected. 'This isn't beer—this is holy water with foam on top!'

Rafid kept making these weird comments and jokes all evening. He talked a lot but it never got tedious. Each additional beer put him even more in the mood, and he radiated friendliness and wit. He was always like that: his presence was usually all it took to put everyone else in a good mood. However, whenever he stopped telling jokes for a second, a deep sadness would suddenly come over his face, but it was wiped away when he started to speak again. I've never questioned him about his past. We all generally talked in very superficial terms about our homes and our families. Nobody wanted to pry, as if the past were a lasting and painful secret. I knew that Rafid must have had a hard life, though. I realized that every night when he began to scream and moan in his sleep. One time he even started to hit himself, then held his hand to his throat and began to force down hard on it. I rushed over to him and woke him from his dream.

'What?' he stammered.

'You must have been having a bad dream.'

'What, *life*?' he shot back with a chuckle. 'You can say that again, my friend: it's the most horrible nightmare there is.'

That evening in the Iraqi Christian Block, a very drunk Rafid was discussing the creation story with a newcomer called Sinan. Whereas Rafid was an inveterate atheist, Sinan believed in the Genesis and the Holy Trinity and looked completely baffled by his futile battle with the slurring sceptic. At one point Rafid went to the toilet and when he came back, he stood in the doorway and said, 'Christians and Muslims are very tolerant towards each other—at least when they're pissing.' We roared with laughter. It warmed our hearts when Rafid said something like that. 'And something else!' he murmured in a voice interrupted by regular belches, as if he were about to throw up. 'I just saw a Coca-Cola bottle on the floor next to a roll of toilet paper. You Christians use the paper, and we wash our arses with water from the cola bottle. So we're in harmony on the toilet, since the toilet roll and the cola bottle are lying alongside each other like old friends. Our cultural exchange is running smoothly, even on the crapper!'

This led on to a discussion about different toilet habits. We accused our Christian hosts of uncleanliness because they didn't wash their backsides with water after defecating.

'Damn, your arses stink!' shouted Rafid. 'Now you know why we Muslims and Jews have had so many run-ins with you Christians over the centuries. We never let you convert us because we don't want to pong like you. In fact, we were only running from your stinking arses during your first Crusades because your knights lifted up their chainmail and charged Jerusalem with their brown arses facing forwards! We had to find some filter masks before we could chase you out of the Islamic world and send you back to your toilet paper in Europe.'

Rafid guffawed, banging the table with his hands. The Christians retorted that we Muslims soiled and wrecked their toilets because we weren't accustomed to sitting on a raised plastic seat.

'All you've ever seen is a hole in the floor, and so here you climb on top of the toilet bowl like barbarians, crouch down and your aim is so bad that half of your shit misses,' said Zechariah. 'We can all tell if a Muslim's been to the toilet before us because we can see your shoe prints on the bowl and the whole floor is wet, or else you've broken the toilet seats because you can't be bothered to put them up. Know what, though? Maybe we should ask the hostel managers to put in some bidets! *We* could sit on them and wipe ourselves with toilet paper afterwards—and *you* could crouch over them and wash your arses with water. That way we'd all be happy!'

By around midnight we were all completely pissed. Zechariah passed me a glass of vodka and said, 'Cheers, Karim, my dear friend! Tell me, have you finally come up with a story?'

Although I was pretty tipsy, I looked at him with irritation. How did he even know I was looking for one?

'No, not yet.'

'Gay would be a good idea!' Rafid suggested, and while there was more loud laughter, he inadvertently grabbed my chest, as if he'd uncovered my secret. I wasn't even gay, but I knew that the others would think I was if they discovered that I was a man-woman.

'No, honestly. Homosexuals have all kinds of rights here, unlike back home where people beat them with sandals. If you tell them you're an Iraqi gay, they'll give you a residence permit straight away. People here know exactly how badly homosexuals are treated in our country. A Tunisian guy who was taken to a different asylum seekers' hostel last month pleaded that he was homosexual, even though he was a massive macho who'd stalk any and every woman. He pretended to be an Iraqi and came up with a heartbreaking account of being queer in Mesopotamia. The judge believed the whole farce and assured him that he would soon get a residence permit. There's even a Nepalese bloke on our floor who's using a gay story. He is truly gay, for a change; he genuinely moves like a woman.'

I felt as if I were being attacked, caught in the act. 'You can't be serious,' I said, trying to be as virile as possible, as if the mere suggestion had wounded my pride.

'I *am* serious. You have six alternatives if you want to convince the judge. Either you've done something against the regime and they're hunting you, or you're a Christian, a communist, a member of a Shiite party, a homosexual or belong to a minority. There are no other options for an Iraqi.'

'Why are you all being so tough on me?'

'Oh come on, let's party!' Rafid said to encourage me. He fetched a cooking pot, balanced it on his thigh and began to drum wildly upon it. The others clapped, and I pummelled the table with my hands. Sinan started to sing: he had a beautiful voice.

Less than five minutes into our concert, two guards suddenly entered the room and demanded our papers. 'You're not allowed to make so much noise. It's forbidden!'

'But today's Friday!' said Zechariah.

'It's the rules. Be quiet!' hissed the guard.

The men inspected our papers and then disappeared again. We were all quiet for a moment.

'Okay,' said Rafid, drumming very quietly on the pot. He gave us a strange look. He started to play more loudly. 'The rules, quiet!' he called, and all of a sudden he hammered like mad on the cooking pot, shouting 'The rules, quiet!', then stood up and began bouncing and dancing around, shouting the words 'the rules' and 'quiet' over and over again. We all joined in with his shouting. We yelled more and more loudly, 'The rules, quiet', and banged on the door and any other object we could find, like monkeys at the zoo. We stamped our feet and barged into each other, and I felt like a member of a sect appealing to its gods in a total trance. 'The rules, quiet!' Deep inside me, I was flooded with a feeling I'd almost forgotten: I felt free. I shut my eyes, banged on the door with my fist—'The rules, quiet!'—stomped and danced—

'The rules, quiet!'—until amid the madness someone shouted, 'Power cut!'

I opened my eyes to find that the room really was pitch-black. One by one, we stopped singing.

'What's going on?' I said. 'This is like being in Iraq.'

'They must have turned off the electricity,' someone said before being interrupted in mid-sentence by the door being flung open and a group of police officers shining their torches in our faces. The party was over. We had to go back to our rooms or else we'd all be arrested, one of the uniformed men told us.

We walked to our rooms. Ali and Salim immediately threw themselves on their mattresses and started to snore. Rafid and I sat down on the floor. We laid the tobacco pouch on a naked blonde's golden bosom and used her colour photo in the *BILD* newspaper as a rolling surface. We chatted quietly and smoked a few cigarettes.

'I know one guy,' I said, 'who made fun of the government once and was immediately arrested. His name's Meki, and he was my friend in year eleven at school.'

'Sounds good. Tell me every detail. Maybe it'll inspire a story for you that meets the legal requirements here!'

I didn't sleep a wink the night before my hearing. I didn't want to disturb my roommates, so I stood fidgeting and smoking in the cold outside our house to while away the time. I tried to block out the real reason for my asylum application. I had now settled on one of the six possible grounds for asylum: I had publicly insulted Saddam Hussein and his wife.

I had taken all my real details—date of birth, schooling, address, etc.—and incorporated them into a new life story. I'd written down loads of notes and learnt them all by heart. It had been surprisingly easy. Once you've come up with a beginning, the other ideas take care of themselves. My only real concern now was that I had to tell this story to a judge. I had to convince him. That was my greatest hurdle.

My appointment was at 8.30 a.m. I arrived at the administrative office quarter of an hour early and sat down outside courtroom number 3, where my hearing was scheduled to take place. I had another few minutes before either the deluge of a temporary stay and then deportation would come crashing down on me, or I would hopefully be saved by a residence permit, my equivalent of Noah's Ark. My entire destiny was in the hands of a single person—the judge waiting inside that room.

A black-haired man of about thirty suddenly appeared in front of me and said in Arabic, 'My name is Omer and I'm your interpreter. You may now enter.'

I went in, and he followed me.

'Sit down!' he ordered a little too curtly.

I sat down at the brown table. The judge, a gaunt, grey-haired man in his early fifties, was already sitting on the other side of it. The interpreter took a seat on the chair to my left. The judge removed his glasses from a silver case, placed them on his hoary nose and glanced at me. He greeted me with a fleeting smile and a 'Good morning!', then switched on a Dictaphone, set it down on the table and began to speak.

'Bayreuth, 21 February 2001. Federal Office for Migration and Refugees. Reference: 2656761563. Hearing for an asylum application. Surname: Mensy. First name: Karim. Date of birth: 12 June 1981. Place of birth: Baghdad.'

He opened a thick red book emblazoned with gold Latin lettering, flicked through it quickly and laid it back down on the table. He then began to talk in a low voice to my interpreter. I couldn't understand what their conversation was about because Omer didn't translate a word of it into Arabic. Their exchange was so conspiratorial that it seemed as if the two men were sharing a secret. I'd spent the whole of the previous night picturing every detail of the hearing. However, the actual setting looked nothing like I'd imagined it. I thought that there would be a hundred police officers there, a public prosecutor taking part in the trial, and a judge wearing a black suit and holding a gavel in his hand, which he would repeatedly bring thundering down on the table top. In my mind the room had been gigantic, with several rows of howling spectators potentially hurling cabbages and tomatoes at me, though I would have dodged them so that they splattered against the fine dark wood-panelled walls. So my judge, *Frau* Schulz, was only half a judge, just as Rafid had told me, and the room didn't resemble a court at all. It was a simple room with a plastic-veneered plywood table, a few wooden chairs, some shelves groaning with files, a clock ticking on the wall and one large window. I could only guess at the window, though, because it was entirely obscured by a yellow curtain. The whole room was bathed in a diffuse light.

'Let us begin. Are you ready?' the interpreter asked me.

My mouth was dry, and it felt as if my tongue were glued to my palate and didn't want to move. I nodded. 'Yes.'

Our conversation lasted exactly eighty minutes. I had to answer forty questions, divided into four categories. Those four categories were personal, grounds for asylum, route and miscellaneous. First, the decision maker wanted to know which languages I spoke, my nationality, to which tribe I belonged and which documents and papers I had as proof of my identity. Then he asked for my official place of residence in my home country and the addresses of my parents, grandparents and brothers and sisters, as if he were planning to send them a greeting card from us both. He also wanted to know if I had any relatives in Europe, if I had a visa for the Federal Republic of Germany and if I was truly Iraqi. He asked me how many cinemas there were in the centre of Baghdad, and I had to name some of them. Where is the university in Baghdad? Where is Baghdad airport? This question bewildered me because I wasn't even sure if there were any international flights in Iraq. All I knew was that, due to the various wars, it had been hard to travel in and out of Iraq since the eighties.

So far, so good: I had only needed to tell the truth. It only became properly tense after that.

'What were your immediate grounds for leaving your country and seeking asylum in Germany?'

'My story is very simple,' I said, relieved to be able to put on the performance I'd so carefully rehearsed. 'A few weeks after our final high-school exams, we assembled in our old classroom, where we were presented with our certificates. Next, we were due to meet all our teachers in the school playground for a celebration. Our old form teacher's name was Hylal, and he was a hard-line nationalist who regarded Saddam as a hero.

'He had always ended his social studies class with a quotation from the president's latest speech, before analysing its content and use of language. But who on earth wanted to listen to Saddam? Every day from 8 p.m. to midnight he would appear on flickering TV screens, harping on about any subject that popped into his head, even cooking and gardening. Sometimes people were invited to praise him or sing and dance for him. In the meantime we dreamt that he might finally clear the screen so we could watch a soap opera.

'On the day of our graduation ceremony, our teacher Hylal told us that he thought it was a shame that we didn't get the chance to analyse the president's wise sayings in our maths lessons, for example. In the euphoria of that day and of receiving the certificate that lay before me on the desk, a fun idea occurred to me and I presented it to the whole class.

'"We can invent a new formula. President Saddam is S1; his wife Sajeda, S2. Multiply them and you get the child or people, CP3. That means that Iraq is a ZERO. Without S1 and S2 there are no children, no people. And without them there is no country and no Iraq. What do you think, sir?"

'The whole class burst out laughing. Our teacher Hylal was the only one not laughing. He stared at me, seething with anger.

'"Are you mocking our president and his wife? How dare you! I'm going to report you to the headmaster this minute."

'He stormed out as if he were going into battle. All my classmates suddenly fell silent and stared at me wide-eyed. We all seemed to be paralysed until one of my classmates finally found his tongue.

'"By Allah, what have you done? Get out of here! If the headmaster hears about this, he'll call the security police and we'll all be shafted! Get out of here, for fuck's sake!"

'I leapt to my feet, grabbed my certificate and rushed out. It was only just becoming clear to me what I had done, and from that moment I was on the run from the government.'

The story wasn't even a lie, *Frau* Schulz. It's a true story, except that it wasn't me who did the prank but my school friend Meki. And it didn't happen on the day we were presented with our certificates, but a year earlier in year eleven. Meki was arrested for it, and nobody has heard from him since. I stole his story and added the happy ending about running away, which Meki unfortunately, and stupidly, didn't do. It was easy to nick his story and make it my own because I was there when it happened. I often wished Meki really had run away, as our classmates had urged him to do, but he seemed numb with fear and simply sat in the classroom until the headmaster sent someone to fetch him. That was the last we saw of Meki.

The decision maker hurled his next major questions about my life at me. 'When and how did you leave your native country? Which means of transport did you use?'

I served up the Istanbul route—the routine story that any halfway sensible Iraqi gives.

'Which countries and cities did you travel to from Turkey?'

'I don't know exactly which countries I travelled through on my way to Germany. I hid in the back of a truck with three other refugees. We couldn't speak to the driver through the back wall of his cab. There were no windows, and so we couldn't see where we were either. We lay or sat there like a cargo of aubergines or oranges. We had enough food with us, as well as a few bags to pee into, which the driver took and threw away in the evenings. When he opened the door at night, it was so dark outside that we could barely see our hands in front of our faces. We always stopped far from any settlements, out in the sticks, and though we did get out every couple of days to stretch our weary legs and do a number two, it was impossible to recognize anything. Some undergrowth in the darkness and a few stones by the side of the road weren't enough to tell me which country I was in at the time. Unfortunately, I'm not good enough at astronavigation to determine my location. Neither can I give any more details about the truck driver who brought us to Germany, other than that I suspect he was Turkish, because we set off from Istanbul. I paid five thousand dollars for the whole journey.'

'What do you have to fear if you return to your native country?'

'I left the country illegally, so I would be punished even more harshly than if I'd stayed. I would be summarily executed.'

'Have you understood the interpreter well throughout this hearing?'

'Yes, very well, in fact,' I claimed, although he spoke pretty wretched Arabic. I could tell by his accent that he was a Kurd. I may have been scared that if I said anything else he wouldn't put in a good word for me with the decision maker.

The judge then read out a short text, which the interpreter translated for me. 'Today I have had a hearing with the Federal Office for Migration and Refugees and was able to present my grounds for seeking asylum. The hearing was taped and translated back to me. The re-translated recording matches the statements I made today. My statements are complete and truthful. The hearing was conducted in Arabic. There were no problems of comprehension. I was then informed that a copy of the transcript of the hearing will be sent to me or to my legal representative.'

My half-judge switched off the Dictaphone and asked me to sign below this text.

Two or three days after the hearing, I was giving Salim a hand with the cooking. As I sat at the common-room table chopping onions and vegetables, I grumbled about the guard at the entrance who was always checking my identity card, even though he knew me. I kept cursing, 'Charab Allmanya!' which means something like 'May Germany be destroyed!' as I cut the garlic so finely that it was reduced to a sticky, yellowy-white mush.

'Karim Charab Allmanya! Stop cursing the whole time and pass me the salt!' said Salim.

Everyone in the kitchen who understood Arabic laughed their heads off. From then on, my real surname was consigned to oblivion. Nobody called me Karim Mensy any more. Instead, all the Iraqis in the hostel called me Karim Charab Allmanya.

'Charab Allmanya!' is a common saying in Iraq, dear *Frau* Schulz, one that people use a lot. If an Iraqi is in a bad mood, he demonizes the Germans for everything that's wrong with the world. Iraqis put all their full feeling into it. Alternatively, some people say, 'Chara be Allmanya!' which roughly equates to 'Shit on Germany'.

As a child I had heard my parents, my siblings, my classmates, my friends and even actors in TV series longing for Germany's demise. I knew next to nothing about Germany as a kid, but of course I parroted what everyone said, without a second thought as to what it meant. I've no idea how that saying became so common in Iraq. Why didn't we curse the Turks, who had ruled our land with an iron fist for more than four hundred years, the English, who had besieged us and toyed with us for years, or the Amcricans, who had bombed our country back into the Stone Age?

Historically, there is, as far as I know, no direct political link between Iraq and Germany, merely minor matters of no lasting consequence. One of those was the Berlin–Baghdad railway line planned at the beginning of last century. Or the Austrian painter Adolf Hitler, who backed the Iraqi nationalists against the British and their Iraqi allies when he was a German politician; the result of that particular cooperation was a failed coup. None of that is of any importance in the broad sweep of Mesopotamian history.

I suspect that the Iraqis learnt this damnation of the Germans from the English. They were the occupying and ruling power in Iraq in the early twentieth century. Maybe the British wanted to impress the Iraqis by cursing their First World War foes in Arabic?

Rafid had a different theory. He thought that demonizing the Germans had nothing to do with the historical context, but was instead a pun. He pointed out that 'Allmanya' sounded like 'Allah', and that people might have wanted to avoid blaspheming when they were angry. So they didn't say 'May Allah be destroyed!' but 'May All—', with a slight pause before '—manya' instead of '—lah'. So, 'Shit on Germany', but not on Allah.

Rafid's theory strikes me as fairly plausible as Iraqis do tend to pause between 'All—' and '—manya' when they use this expression. So it may well merely be a linguistic game. Poor Germans, they have no inkling that every day people insult and damn them in a distant land for no reason.

Dear *Frau* Schulz, I didn't actually use 'Charab Allmanya!' that much before. I've never sworn so much in my whole life as in the days and weeks following my hearing. After all, I had nothing to do but wait for its outcome. Despite knowing that the decision, to be made in Nuremberg, might take months and even years, I waited in my room every Monday, Wednesday and Friday from 8 a.m. to 2 p.m. and every Tuesday and Thursday from 1 p.m. to 6 p.m. for the caretaker, as he was also the hostel postman. We didn't have our own letterbox or pigeonholes, so he would bring us our letters when he came by to do some repairs. We all looked expectantly at him as he came ambling along the corridor in his overalls, a pile of letters in one hand and his heavy silver-grey toolbox in the other.

Our lot called this nice man Azrael, who was generally very taciturn, Malik al-Maut—the Angel of Death. I don't know who gave him that nickname, but he had done absolutely nothing to deserve it. When I first heard the name I remembered that my mother had once told me about my brother who'd died in childbirth. 'He had to go straight back to heaven,' she explained, 'so he can become a child angel. He will protect us and defend us from God's judgement in heaven. When they die, babies become their parents' guardian angels in the afterlife. And in *djanna*, in paradise, they are birds, and they will wake us in the mornings with their magnificent song.'

But Azrael isn't a child angel. In our mythology he is the angel of death, the one who keeps a record of all the newborn babies and strikes the names of the dead from the list of the living. He is said to have two faces—an ugly grimace and a beautiful countenance. To those who enter paradise he allegedly shows his nice face, and to the others the face of a ghoul. They claim that one day he will come for me, for everyone—yes, even for you, *Frau* Schulz.

Before I lived in an asylum seekers' hostel, I thought that if he ever appeared, he would only come to me as I lay dying. Yet in Bayreuth I met him five times per week in the form of a German caretaker called *Herr* Hubert, who went around the house delivering letters. *Herr* Hubert's features always displayed the same mixture of irritation, agitation and fatigue. The asylum seekers' faces could look very different, though. They would beam with joy or twist with pain, depending on the type of letter *Herr* Hubert conveyed. Every day I waited for the green envelope from Nuremberg that would determine my own expression. My story had actually lifted my spirits, but I was petrified every time I saw Azrael—Malik al-Maut—in the corridor.

I dreamt of all the things I would do if I were granted a residence permit. I began to spin these plans further and further into the future. I imagined a new life as a free man. I would find a surgeon to bestow a flat chest on me and would at last be able to wear tight clothing and walk through the streets with my head held high. I would get a place at university and find a pretty fellow student to be my girlfriend, with whom I would even be able to converse in German after a short while. Soon I would have a well-paid job for an international company based in a glass-and-steel skyscraper, and from my spacious office I would look out over the roofs of the city. I would bring my parents over from Iraq and buy myself a house beside the sea, and in the summer all of us—my father, my mother and my university sweetheart—would go there on holiday. Our faces would be as happy and peaceful as the expressions on soft toys.

Yet Azrael didn't bring me any news for a long time, a very long time. When he did at last appear in my doorway one day, he pressed a green envelope into my hand without comment. All it contained, though, was the re-translated text of my hearing for my files. My days passed at a snail's pace, as if a cosmic force were kneading time like pizza dough, rolling it out as thinly as possible.

We were, dear *Frau* Schulz, a bunch of twitchy birds, waiting either for their court hearing or the results of their asylum application, unsure what might become of us. We were paralysed by shock and felt like the statues by the Markgrafen fountain in the town centre, slowly gathering moss. Our everyday life consisted of boredom interspersed with groundless arguments and various inexplicable conflicts.

One day, for example, a Pakistani by the name of Salman demanded to be taken to new accommodation. He called the police, claiming that his housemates were spies and not the Indians they pretended to be; they worked for the ISI, the Pakistani secret service. Caritas did actually intervene in this diplomatic incident, and Salman was given a new bed in the Afghan room on the same corridor. So he moved to a different room in the Orient Express. It took less than a day for the next problem to crop up, though: his new roommates allegedly tied him to his bed and even beat him.

Salman often bothered the hostel's other residents by hanging around in the common kitchen and weeping bitterly, as if he'd just discovered that his whole family had died and that he'd also contracted a fatal disease. It was practically impossible to find out what was really wrong and if someone might be able to help him; he probably didn't even know himself. Then, one day, he simply vanished from the hostel, as if the ground had swallowed him up. He must have either done a bunk or been moved because of his constant quarrelling.

Meanwhile, another refugee called Idris, who lived on the Kurdish floor, became a big problem for the Arabs. I'd met this kid before, *Frau* Schulz: he was one of the three lads the smuggler dropped off in Dachau with me. Like me, he had ended up in Bayreuth. The poor guy almost went out of his mind when his asylum application was rejected with surprising speed. Clutching the crumpled letter in his hand, he suddenly began to scream, cry and punch himself in the face and lashing out at the door and the furniture in his room like a dervish. When he had calmed down—or rather fatigue and the pain of his battered hands had sapped all his furious energy—he would no longer speak Arabic to us Arabs, or so much as look at an Arab. Instead, every time he caught an Arab on the Kurdish floor, he would immediately attack them. We found this extremely racist, of course, and discussed it for days with his fellow Kurds, pointing out in particular that we Arabs had nothing to do with the rejection of his application.

The Kurds eventually decided that strangers could only enter their floor of the building by prior arrangement. We had to warn them before any visit so that someone could restrain or distract Idris the Kurd. For almost three weeks that floor was out of bounds until Idris the hothead was eventually relocated and probably deported.

Occasionally, during our long wait, there were problems that made us asylum seekers laugh, but annoyed the locals and the police. For example, two Africans and a Syrian went into a restaurant one day and ordered a huge slab of meat. They ate it and then did a runner without paying the bill. Of course, everyone knew where to find them. The police and the waitress searched the whole hostel for them, but we all looked the same to the girl, or at least the black Africans did. She identified nine suspects for the police, but of them only the Syrian was actually guilty. So the two Africans decided of their own accord to hand themselves in, and the three of them ultimately got off with a caution and an order to apologize.

From time to time some of us were caught shoplifting in the supermarket or in Rotmain. The people of Bayreuth, who seemed pretty fed up with us refugees, had grown familiar with this game over the years. Many of them simply didn't let any more refugees into their shops or watched us for so long and so obtrusively that we immediately left. I felt as if I was surrounded by people bent on reporting me for the slightest misdemeanour. I felt like a convicted offender who is supposed to be undergoing rehabilitation in a small town where all the inhabitants are aware of his crime.

Conflicts broke out on an almost hourly basis at the hostel. Again and again, someone would claim that someone else had stolen something from a state food parcel. These arguments often concluded with a brawl or with the police being called. In the Orient Express, on the other hand, disputes were often caused by women, although the women themselves were never present and generally thousands of miles away. But someone had verbally fucked someone else's sister or mother, and fighting or a stabbing quickly ensued.

There was always lots going on, and yet life remained unspeakably boring. We could do nothing but wait, and every passing day dulled our wits a little more.

Always seeing the same faces in the hostel nagged at us too. We all yearned for a little variety. When the hostel was full, no new refugees arrived for quite a while. I dearly wanted some contact with people from Bayreuth, but the only regular encounters we had with Germans, other than disparaging glances, were with police officers or the hostel guards—that is, with people whose jobs dictated that they couldn't ignore us. All other regular citizens were like mythical creatures from a remote fairy-tale land that we observed on one of our forays into town or through the fence around the hostel. Smart-looking, fair-skinned people of all shapes and sizes, swaddled in thick, warm, beautiful clothes. Clean children, pretty mothers, proud fathers. When I tried to follow their conversations and learn a bit of German, all I could hear was 'sh . . . shi . . . k . . . ko . . . ' The words sounds like interference on a radio that needs tuning. It's a real challenge to learn German by straining to catch the odd word spoken by passers-by in a northern Bavarian town.

The only Germans without batons and firearms who stayed in our vicinity of their own volition and for any length of time were the Caritas staff members. One of these was Karin Schmitt, the woman who had helped me to find a few items of warm clothing when I first arrived. She worked for the charity on a voluntary basis and mixed with us every day. People called her 'the lady with the box'. She was our Father Christmas, without the beard and red bobble hat, because every morning she brought a boxful of second-hand clothes, magazines, old crockery, cutlery and other things that made our daily lives easier.

However, Karin did the rounds of the families first before coming to see us single men with the meagre remains. Afterwards, the empty box stood for the rest of the day outside the Caritas office, and we could walk past and have a look to see whether anything useful had landed in it in the meantime. Female activists from Bayreuth would occasionally come to the hostel and donate various unwanted objects to Caritas so we might benefit from items that would otherwise have been thrown away or have gathered dust in a cellar or attic.

Yet Karin Schmitt was more to us than merely the 'lady with the box'.

Her face was deathly pale, and she would apply a modicum of powder only for official engagements. She would coat her chapped lips, which were always dry, with lip balm or with burgundy lipstick for special occasions. Her features reminded me of an advert for a French cookbook I'd once seen in a German women's magazine. The picture showed a slightly rare veal steak, cut open and served with fried onions and a few drops of light-yellow sauce. The white-aproned chef presenting it looked a lot like *Frau* Schmitt. She had shoulder-length curls and big brown eyes. Beyond her appearance, though, I couldn't really fathom Karin. Unable to figure her out, I wondered what precisely this woman wanted from life. All we knew was that she loved 'us'. She sacrificed herself for us complete strangers, as if we were her relatives. She lent a sympathetic ear to our troubles with our asylum applications and other everyday occurrences. Although most of our problems were intractable, she had a knack for calming us down and giving us hope when the prospects seemed desperate to us. She gave the impression that she was completely devoted to helping and standing up for us whenever the authorities caught us off guard or crushed our dreams and souls into the dust like steamrollers. Karin Schmitt dedicated so much time to this unpaid work that she might as well have moved in with us.

Maybe, secretly, she would have felt lonely and alone without us refugees; maybe she didn't have any relatives or at least no close ties to her family. Her life may have been deadly dull, and our problems lent some spice to her days. We presumably made her feel important and needed. Once she made a remark that caused a short-lived outbreak of speculation among us men.

'Along with Nora, you are my true family.'

This ominous Nora was apparently the only person of any importance in her life apart from the hostel residents. We thought Nora must be a woman, but one day we all found out who she really was—a horse. This animal seemed to be Karin's sole hobby, and whenever she had time she would drive out to the countryside to see Nora. She never mentioned any other relatives or friends.

One day, though, brought a major change. It happened during a party Karin had organized at the hostel for two Iraqi lads. Shortly beforehand, they had been granted permission to visit their uncle and live with him in Nuremberg until the result of their asylum application was known. They had never previously been allowed to leave Bayreuth due to the mandatory residence rule, but their uncle had apparently got them a good lawyer who had pushed it through.

One of the lads was called Haider, and what he told us at the party sounded absurd. 'We crossed ten countries on foot, having all kinds of experiences, and danger became part of our daily lives. Then we got here and suddenly we weren't even allowed to visit our uncle in Nuremberg only a few miles away. Just an hour by train from here. It's crazy. I don't get it, but that's the law. Now, at last, we can leave Bayreuth, the hostel and you lot, you old fart-breaths! But you know what they call Nuremberg?'

'No, what?' someone called out.

'Kurdemberg, because so many Kurds live there. From tomorrow we're Kurdembergers, not Iraqi Bayreuthers any more.'

We had a fun time with those two happy lads that evening. I was jealous, though, that they would now be living in a big city and were even allowed to travel around. I wanted to be able to do the same.

Their uncle had sent some money so that we could buy some cake, soft drinks, beer and wine. The two lads celebrated, laughing and dancing. Everyone was in a good mood, even Karin Schmitt. Then the party came to a dramatic end. Ali was to blame—Ali of all people, a deeply religious man who usually spoke to no one but Allah. He suddenly leapt out of his chair and demanded that Rafid translate, word for word, everything that he wanted to say to Karin. We all fell silent and listened. Ali waited for a moment, cleared his throat and then began his speech in Arabic.

'Karin, you are a wonderful person. Nobody really took care of us here, only you. For us you are like a mother and a sister rolled into one. Thank you too for arranging this party for the boys. I don't think it's fair that you live alone with a horse called Nora. I would like to marry you. We could found a small family and have children who play with Nora.'

When Rafid had translated the last word, we all burst out laughing, roaring with delight. Yet Karin just stood there, rooted to the spot, seemingly overwhelmed by the situation.

Ali was deeply hurt by our reaction. 'Why are you morons laughing? Don't you have hearts? I'm serious.'

Somehow the situation got out of hand. We cheered, Ali stomped around in circles and Karin ran out to her car in tears and drove away. The party was over. Nobody felt like celebrating any more that evening. Yet the event made Ali and Karin hostel legends, stars of a grand romance.

Ali was a simple boy and, as I've already mentioned, a deeply religious one. We usually just called him 'Dumpster Ali' because he was permanently scouring the town's refuse containers on the lookout for anything useful. He was half Iraqi and half Persian or maybe neither; he didn't really know himself. During the Iran–Iraq War, when he was still a kid, his family was deported to Iran because the Iraqi government regarded them as Persians and therefore treated them as racially impure Iraqis, even though Ali's folk had lived in Iraq since the eighteenth century. The Iranians, however, saw them as Iraqis and hence racially impure Persians. For almost his entire childhood he and his family lived in a kind of detention camp, completely cut off from the outside world. He didn't attend school and therefore had almost no knowledge of Iraq or Iran, or anything else for that matter. Actually, the only things he knew anything about were Allah and dumpsters.

Along his route he had rummaged in all sorts of dumpsters, from Iran to Germany via Turkey, Greece and Italy. He was an absolute expert in his field. His father had been a major businessman in Iraq, and he too had dealt with refuse. Before the war he had sealed a deal with the Interior Ministry to empty all the bins in Baghdad's prisons and dispose of the waste. He was viewed as an important figure and considered himself a loyal government supporter. Yet reality had a different fate in mind for him.

Years later, in an Iranian camp, Ali's father would stand outside the office distributing bread and other food items every day and stare at the dumpsters which contained nothing useful, only residual waste. He made several business propositions relating to waste disposal to the camp's administrators, but no one was interested. When he attempted to offer his services to the Iraqi opposition, which cooperated with the Iranians, his past support for the regime proved a stain on his name. He felt alone and abandoned. He would take his son on a daily tour of the dumpsters and they would forage for anything reusable. Ali's father later died of sadness and rootlessness.

Ali never stopped rummaging in dumpsters. On his escape route to Germany through many countries, he got to know of the different waste disposal arrangements, and he was now familiar with Bayreuth's rubbish system. Of course, refuse disposal is a specialist science in Germany, with any number of different colours and symbols for specific types of waste, but Ali probably knew his way around it better that most native Germans. He was easy to find if he went missing: you just visited the various collection points around town equipped with large dumpsters. Ali always returned from his excursions with something useful. Rafid, Salim and I generally left him in peace, and he was grateful that we didn't make fun of him.

Ali, whom nobody had taken care of for so long, had not only entrusted his fate to Allah but had also fallen in love with kindly Karin. It was clear to everyone at the aforementioned party that he really did want her to be his wife. He had often talked about her and raved about what a fantastic woman she was, but I'd never have imagined that he would pluck up the courage to tell her to her face. I later found out that someone at the party had tricked him into drinking some wine by pretending that it was grape juice. Having never tasted wine out of fear of Allah, Ali was so glad to drink something other than water for once that he drained a whole glass. Boy, did he love that grape juice.

The rest is history. Karin, who was twenty years his senior, turned down his marriage proposal, but that was far from the end of it. From then on Ali presented her with roses each week. Every Friday, during her lunch break, he would bring her a red rose and lay it down in front of her office door. He would wait until she left her office in the afternoon and walk behind her to the car park, then wave as she drove away.

Probably scared, Karin never wanted anything to do with Ali again. Then one day we heard that she didn't work at the hostel any more. She simply disappeared from our lives, like the sun during a German winter.

On that day, dear *Frau* Schulz, Ali laid no rose outside the Caritas office. Instead, he dragged every bin in the hostel to the front of the office and emptied them out onto the ground. He carried on doing this until the security guards came and arrested him amid the filth. He spent the night in police custody.

Dear *Frau* Schulz, it was one rainy day in April when I heard that the time had come for me to bid Bayreuth farewell. I was sitting in our room, bored, flicking through a magazine called *Freundin* I had brought back from Caritas. It is full of photos of skinny, half-naked women without a wrinkle, and even the men who occasionally feature in its pages look perfectly flawless, like the Greek gods on Mount Olympus. Suddenly there was a knock on the door. It was Azrael, the caretaker angel. He pressed a letter into my hand.

The envelope was green. I thought it was the result of my asylum application, but it was actually only a short text, stamped and signed. I didn't understand a word. I hurried out of the room to find Rafid and ask him to translate it for me. He was standing outside the kitchen with Salim, Ali and a few other Iraqis.

'Oh dear, a green letter. The colour of the Prophet Muhammad *and* the most powerful German authorities. Let me take a look!'

Quite a number of us seemed to have received the same message that day. It said that we were to pack up our belongings because we were going to be moved at nine o'clock the next morning. There wasn't a word about where we were going, and no reason was given for our transfer. I wanted to go and see Caritas straight away to ask for the name of my future place of residence. Rafid said that he'd already tried to find out, but none of the staff were there any more.

'This could be our last evening together in Bayreuth,' said Salim. 'Let's cook something! Our last supper in Bayreuth! Who knows, maybe they'll take us to different hostels tomorrow. Let's throw a farewell party! With rice and tomato sauce!'

Salim was a passionate cook. Every week, when we received the food parcels, he would try to swap some of the contents with the Yugoslavs and the Kazaks. That's because there were many things in the packages that we didn't eat: salami, pasta, ready meals and canned soup, coloured hardboiled eggs and those weird yellow things—fish fingers. In return for them Salim got beans, rice and vegetables. He never managed to arrange any poultry or red meat, though; that kind of thing was seen as the height of luxury, and we had eaten virtually none since we'd become refugees. Only once in the past weeks had we come across any meat in one of the food parcels. The minced beef may no longer have been red, having turned a shade of brown, but Salim nonetheless conjured up three wonderful dishes from that little bit of mince: meatballs, meat sauce and another mince creation so unusual that I can barely describe it in retrospect. After that, we saw no more of the meat we craved and so we remained reluctant vegetarians.

Salim was able to conjure a great meal out of nothing. There was a story to his cooking skills, which he enjoyed telling at great length, forcing it on the ears of every newcomer to our floor. It was the only aspect of his past that he was prepared to explain in any detail. He was otherwise a taciturn, placid man, and that's why we called him Salim the Silent.

He had left Iraq at the age of twenty-five because he hadn't been able to find a job after studying economics. The country was suffering from a trade embargo, and in addition Salim was suffering because of his father, whom he could no longer stand. The government charged two thousand dollars for a passport, so he opted for a less financially onerous variant and tried to leave the country for Syria with the help of the Kurds in the north. This fun and games cost him five hundred dollars, which he was just about able to scrape together. When he arrived in Damascus he didn't know how to make tea or fry an egg, but not because he didn't have any money left—he simply didn't know how to. There were too many women in his family back in Baghdad. Salim had been surrounded by four sisters, his mother, his grandmother and his brothers' wives, meaning that he'd never washed a dish, ironed a shirt, polished a shoe or even made tea in his life. At the time he didn't even know what the word 'pepper' meant or what yoghurt was doing in yoghurt soup, although he loved both and ate them daily.

Salim got a job in a factory producing children's toys. He took care of its finances, but his wages were very low compared with those of Syrians—so-called foreign wages. He got through this period by buying cheap snacks like falafel, hummus and ful or makali from stands, while at home he ate virtually nothing but beans, fish and other tinned foods because he wasn't capable of cooking anything else.

After several months, he heard of two countries that issued visas to Iraqis and even guaranteed them a job. Even back then in the early nineties, *Frau* Schulz, the Mesopotamians were unwanted guests in almost every country on earth. Only in Libya and Yemen were they welcome. Salim applied to an agency that found work only for Iraqis and he did indeed get a job as a financial manager for an oil company near Sana'a. On arrival he initially maintained his loyalty to fast food, but later he got to know some fellow Iraqis. Altogether there were six Iraqi families living in that area, so everyone knew everybody and they formed a close-knit community. As the only unmarried man, Salim was often invited to the others' homes for meals. This was the best thing that could have happened to him. He played fondly with the cuddly babies and was spoilt with Iraqi delicacies as he had been back home in Baghdad.

Once, one of Salim's hosts joked that it was high time Salim stopped eating his family out of house and home and finally learnt to cook. Everyone in the room laughed, and Salim also found the idea amusing. Yet one of the women present didn't take it in jest and made a suggestion.

'We women get together once a week to cook, so Salim could learn the secrets of Iraqi cuisine from us if he likes.'

Amazingly, Salim immediately agreed, although he didn't have the foggiest idea of what he was letting himself in for. The offer struck him as a great honour and sign of trust, as men were usually barred from the kitchen.

And so Salim learnt the art of cookery. From the very start, playing with spices, vegetables, flour and meat captivated him. It became such an all-engrossing passion that he soon began inventing his own recipes, which he named after himself and numbered chronologically.

Salim I to XII were famous in the asylum seekers' hostel, even though he could only do approximations of the dishes for lack of Iraqi ingredients. Personally, I liked Salim VII the best: potato wedges with onions, lemon juice, black pepper and olive oil, covered with feta cheese and baked in the oven.

When, after a year, Salim's contract with the oil company was not extended, he quit Yemen and looked for a new home. At the end of an odyssey through various countries, he reached Germany and became our head chef in Bayreuth. This may not have been a paid job, but it certainly wasn't the end of Salim's exploration of world cuisine. He always claimed that he felt like a sultan when standing at the stove. Cooking was neither a job nor a hobby: it was an attitude to life.

Nevertheless, our last supper in Bayreuth was more of a mourning feast than a farewell party. We barely spoke to each other, eating in silence, each contemplating his personal fears and hopes. Our greatest fear was that we would be dragged off to the middle of nowhere. To a mountaintop like the one I'd seen on my journey from Munich to Zirndorf, for example. We hoped for the opposite—to be sent to a real city. A big city, where we might be free to move around as we wished.

When our bus left Bayreuth the next morning, we still didn't know where we were being taken. We were twenty-two men and three women, as well as the driver and an escort. We enquired about our destination but they replied that they didn't know either, which was of course total rubbish. They didn't seem to want to tell us, and that scared us. The two of them hardly looked at us and whispered to each other a great deal.

After a two-hour drive the women had to get out in the middle of the countryside. We had reached their future hostel. In line with every cliché in the book, they were the only ones who had any real luggage with them—four suitcases and all kinds of carrier bags and plastic bags so crammed with belongings that they looked as if they were going to burst at any moment. We men all had tiny rucksacks, and a few didn't even have that much.

A few hundred yards along the road, in an equally depressing spot, we offloaded a Somali, an Albanian and two Pakistanis. There were now only Iraqis left in the bus. We drove on for quite a while before I glimpsed in the distance a small town, surrounded by divine mountain scenery.

'Niederhofen an der Donau, our terminus,' called the driver.

Most of the men, including Ali and Salim, got off and were taken to a house in the centre of the small town. Three blokes, Rafid and I had to wait in the bus. We were driven to the edge of town, where the second lot of asylum seekers' accommodation lay on the banks of a river. It was in an ordinary four-storey building with two flats on each floor. On the ground floor there was a small office where the caretaker was sitting. He sent Rafid and me up to the third floor. We entered our room and were extremely surprised by what we found there. There was a sofa, a table, two beds and a TV; the tiny kitchen was even equipped with crockery. The people who'd lived there before us must have been very tidy.

We put down our things and immediately went back outside to take a look around and visit the town centre, which was a fifteen-minute walk from our new home. We ran into Salim and Ali in the pedestrian zone outside the town hall. We embraced and hugged so heartily that you'd have thought we hadn't seen each other in years. Then we carried on together.

Niederhofen an der Donau is a small town, and many parts of it are very pretty. There's a river with gorgeous banks. A castle on a hill. Narrow, winding lanes. Old half-timbered houses. Tiny, exotic shops and large department stores. Nice cafes and pubs. A university. Lots of young people. To our great delight we even came across the odd kebab shop.

Kebab shops were a good sign. We asylum seekers had a Germany-wide ranking of different towns. Anyone who had any information, even mere hearsay, could participate. The Kebab Shop Index showed how many Turks or other foreigners were living in a particular place, and to us that was in itself an important criterion for determining a town's appeal. Niederhofen did surprisingly well, but Berlin was top of the Kebab Shop Index and, therefore, everyone's dream destination.

It was evening by the time Rafid and I got back to the hostel. We were both impressed by the pretty town and by the many young people and students livening the place up.

As we reached our floor, we met our neighbours for the first time. They were standing around outside the communal bathroom and toilets. We all introduced ourselves. There were three of them—two Kurds and a Turkmen from Iraq. They were to be our first nightmare in this seemingly peaceful place.

We soon christened them the H&M Gang, although they also shoplifted from C&A. The three of them would hang out every afternoon from Monday to Saturday outside H&M and C&A, dripping with fashionable jewellery, hair gelled back, wearing wide, studded belts, gleaming Chinese rip-offs of American sneakers and dark fake-leather or khaki jackets. They looked like cartoon gangsters from mafia B-movies, standing there conspiratorially, scanning the passers-by with piercing looks.

Hewe, Foad and Sargon were our hostel's big shots. Their gang was better known and more ubiquitous than the German flag. All of us, including the town's homeless people, students, potheads, hotheads and alcoholics knew this lot. You must have seen them before too, *Frau* Schulz. And Rafid and I lived on the same floor as them and shat in the same loo.

There was a constant rumpus going on in their flat. They threw regular parties, drank too much and had so many visitors all day, every day, that you would have thought they ran a brothel. We seldom got any peace when they were in their room. Only in the mornings, once they'd gone to bed, did the house fall silent.

These three lads had claimed H&M, C&A and the surrounding area as their turf. Somehow, despite standing outside in plain view, and although the goods were tagged, they still managed to shoplift on a regular basis and flog the stuff at half price on the street. None of them had a residence permit and yet they seemed to be swimming in money. Rumour had it that they were backed by a powerful Polish German mobster and were somehow involved in his drug dealing. If anyone refused to go along with their game and flouted their rules, for example by interfering in their schemes, he would get beaten up. This happened to a Moroccan guy called Mohammed living in the homeless hostel. He once tried to steal a shirt from H&M but was caught by the store detective. The three gangsters immediately got wind of this, and when the police released Mohammed, they gave the poor devil a thrashing. He had intended to keep the stolen shirt for himself, not sell it, but the H&M Gang saw his deed as trespassing on their turf.

Hewe was their leader. He'd been arrested several times already. One time he'd broken a young man's nose for flirting with his flame, Claudia. He spent a few days in jail on the back of that.

Claudia, Anna and Birgit were the H&M Gang's girlfriends. All three were doing some course or other at a vocational college. They were regulars on our floor; we felt as if they lived in the hostel too. Claudia was blonde and didn't say much, though she always had a cheerful smile on her face. Birgit, on the other hand, had black hair and stumpy legs and was very fat. Anna also had an impossible figure. She had virtually no neck, so her head was perched directly on her shoulders. What's more, she had a huge backside and a drooping belly, but no bust. Their parents were all from Eastern Europe, though I don't know which part. Probably from the Czech Republic or Poland. The three girls had been born here, however, so they were true Niederhofeners.

I don't know any more about the three girlfriends because my German wasn't good enough to hold a conversation with them. Yet even if it had been, it would have been practically impossible to find out any more information about them, since they hung out with the H&M Gang every evening and all weekend. Occasionally they would even bring along to our hostel other young girls who felt like partying and smoking dope.

I admit, my dear *Frau* Schulz, that I was often envious of those boys, for they had money and women. By comparison I was a total loser in both departments. That was largely down to my situation, though. How was I supposed to flirt with a woman and take her out without any real knowledge of German and no money? I never went into any of the town's four discos. I tried to a few times, but they would never let me in, so I soon gave up. First, I didn't fancy being treated like dirt by the bouncers, and second, I was worried anyway that my breasts would jiggle too much as I danced. I had to be careful at all times, even in our flat. There were no doors in the shower rooms in the Niederhofen hostel. I would creep into the bathroom like a thief every time, shower for a few seconds and hope nobody walked in on me.

Brawls broke out regularly in our hostel. Hewe was well known for his aggression and could go mental at the flick of a switch. On the odd occasions when he spoke, he would pronounce wise sayings he'd picked up on the streets like 'Actions speak louder than words.' His actions generally involved his fists and his favourite toy—an army knife.

He once got into an argument with a girl who hung out with the local Serbian gang. She told her clan, and it all ended in a fight. He beat up three of the Serbs in the middle of the pedestrian zone before pulling out his dagger. The situation had suddenly got a whole lot more serious, and the Serbs ran away. Hewe stood there, rooted to the spot, scratching his crotch through his jeans with the tip of his army knife. By this time, passers-by had alerted the police, and Hewe offered no resistance as they arrested him. His photo was in the next day's edition of the local newspaper. He was immensely proud of it and pinned the article to the wall above his bed.

He paid for this incident with four weeks in prison. I can only assume, dear *Frau* Schulz, that he had passed himself off as an Iraqi Arab when applying for asylum. There was no other explanation, for otherwise, even before the fall of Saddam, he would have been deported to northern Iraq as a Kurd and a repeat offender. But you know better than I do how your weird laws work.

After his release he threw a party in his room and invited everyone in the hostel round. There was food and large quantities of vodka. I was surprised to hear how good Hewe's German had become all of a sudden. Before his prison sentence he'd had trouble pronouncing most words, but now he could speak pretty fluently. Hewe told us that all the other prison inmates had been German.

'It's a great place to learn German. Here at the hostel, I'm surrounded by idiots like you!'

It was crazy, but studying the other asylum seekers' faces I got the impression that we all dreamt of doing a short spell in jail in order to learn German quickly.

The people of Niederhofen played a greater role in our lives than the locals had in Bayreuth. You, *Frau* Schulz, were one of the first people we saw on a regular basis.

You always look on edge and stressed out, as if you've constantly got your period, with abdominal pains and all the rest of it. A mere mention of your name and a glum mood came over us all. That must be because you're in charge of everything that makes our lives easier or tougher: residence permits, identity cards, work, deportation decisions, pocket money—eighty euros, later reduced to forty—and doctor's certificates.

The only person we like in your administration is *Frau* Richter. Everyone knows her office is the best. She sits there and sincerely and actively tries to come up with a real solution to our problems. All you and the other officials ever say, on the other hand, is 'That's the law!' or 'Come back next week!'

Do you know what room roulette is, *Frau* Schulz? Room roulette is a game that begins when you draw your number and ends when you're called into a room. Whether things get done or not depends on which civil servant's name comes up. It means that if one of you civil servants is in the doghouse with his wife or is dying for a fart, he'll make life tough for us foreigners. Every visit to your offices is a lottery.

And you, *Frau* Schulz—you're one of those people who blow up even the most trivial detail into an affair of state, whereas *Frau* Richter makes lots of things suddenly appear incredibly simple. Every time I stood here at the information desk in the foreigners' registration office, I could see our lot anxiously shifting about on the benches and praying to Allah that they didn't wind up in your office. *Frau* Richter, on the other hand, smiles at each and every one of us when she speaks to us, and she has something that you and all your male colleagues lack—sympathy.

I'm losing my cool. I need to roll myself another joint. You don't mind?

Another German we saw on a regular basis because he appeared twice a week in our hostel was our new Azrael, the caretaker. Like his colleague in Bayreuth, he delivered the mail and our weekly food parcel. He always stayed for exactly four hours. Occasionally he would try to mend something in our dilapidated old house, but he would always stop working again very quickly to go off and look for other spots to repair, and then, after exactly four hours, downed tools and went home.

Various police officers often turned up at our place as well. If anything was stolen in town, the first place they would search was our hostel.

However, the most important people in our lives, *Frau* Schulz, were neither you nor Azrael nor the police. The most important people were the weekend visitors. On Saturdays and Sundays they would either stand directly outside our front door or stroll along the riverbank, keeping an eye out to see if one of us happened to emerge. If a refugee did step out of the house, they would eye him up like a nice juicy hunk of meat in the local butcher's display counter.

These weekend visitors have money. They are generous, always eat out in restaurants and have a high time in cocktail bars. Their shoes are from Italy, their expensive fragrances from France, and their clothes are made by luxury brands like Chanel. They go on holiday to faraway countries. Their apartments are furnished with all the splendour of one of Saddam's presidential palaces and are stocked with crates of drinks and tinned foods in a separate larder. They not only have a shower but also a bathtub and a guest toilet. The bedroom contains a disproportionately large bed, big enough for my whole family to sleep in. Some even own Buddha statues and Persian rugs, and they go on and on about creating a 'Mediterranean feel'.

I never got involved with the weekend visitors and only know about them second-hand. From our first weekend in Niederhofen, it was clear to me what these men and women wanted from us and why they hung around in our vicinity. There were three different categories. They were either drug dealers looking for new workmates, elderly ladies and gentlemen who fancied picking up a young foreign man or pimps on the lookout for fresh blood to supply to their regular clients.

Khaled, a housemate of ours whom we called Khaled the Loverman, was a favourite toy boy of elderly ladies and gentlemen in Niederhofen. When I found out, I suddenly understood why he was always out at night, how he'd made so much money and why he wanted nothing to do with the rest of us. He would sometimes look the other way while sitting in a cafe and seeing us loiter in the street outside, presumably because he thought we might ruin his business. Khaled did all of this for love—not for the elderly ladies, but for a young cultural studies student with whom he'd fallen head over heels. It cost him a pretty penny to invite her to the pizzeria, pay for her drinks and buy clothes and jewellery for her.

A Libyan called Musa also got involved with the ladies. One Saturday he left with one of the German visitors, reappearing only on Tuesday. We could scarcely believe our eyes. He had a new hairstyle, looked well kept and was wearing a leather jacket, new jeans and black Italian shoes. He said that he'd had sex with the woman, and though it took some effort on his part, it really hadn't been so bad: you just had to close your eyes and gyrate your pelvis. He was ready to do it all over again.

'I'd even be willing to live with an old trout like her. Better than rotting away in this hostel.'

We seldom saw him after that; it was as if he'd moved house. He too became a popular lover, and ladies kept coming around, asking after him.

Besides Khaled and Musa, six other lads had dealings with our weekend visitors. It was easy to find out who was getting a piece of the action, for any of us who could afford several beers or kebabs each week must have been earning a bit on the side like this, or else they'd been stealing. There was no other possible explanation.

I never thought that I too would one day have a strange encounter with a weekend visitor.

It all came about because Khaled got his residence permit that summer and decided to leave his weekend visitors and his student girlfriend behind and move to Nuremberg to look for a proper job. As he was saying goodbye, he gave me his mobile number and invited me to visit him if I was ever allowed to travel. I thanked him, somewhat surprised because we hardly knew each other.

A few days after Khaled had left Niederhofen, a car drew up alongside me out of the blue. I gawped at the luxury car, as I'd never seen such a magnificent vehicle at such close quarters before. It must have been a real Ferrari. A man was at the wheel and a small cat was staring out at me suspiciously from the passenger seat. Its white coat was shaggy, but it appeared to have been combed by hand and shone as if newly oiled. Its collar, which was barely visible under its long hair, was made of dazzling red leather and encrusted with gemstones. The animal was sitting on a little blanket, looking incredibly idle and bored. I would later find out that this was a long-haired variety of the British Shorthair. The very name makes it sound like some English lord, and that seemed to be more or less how the cat was treated. Judging by its expression, the cat appeared thoroughly aware of its status.

'It's me! Get in!'

'What? Who you are?'

The man was otherwise rather pale, but he had rouge on his face. I couldn't really work out if his cheeks were chubby or flabby, and it was hard to tell his age. In any case, his appearance was surreal, right down to his pearly white porcelain teeth. His teased-out hair was so blond that it was almost yellow. I wasn't sure whether he was wearing a wig or if he might even have hair implants. Everything down to his beard and his eyebrows looked fake.

He was dressed in a white suit, tailored from fine, gleaming fabric and shimmering a full spectrum of different shades, with a black shirt underneath. He'd positioned a pink silk handkerchief in the breast pocket of his jacket. He was quite small and no fatso, but still looked very stout. His neck only just protruded from his shirt collar, and I was amazed that he could breathe in his buttoned-up shirt. His fingers were fat, compressed and throttled by many rings set with brilliants.

'I've paid for our date.'

'I not understand German very well. What paid?'

'Khaled.' The man now removed his mirrored aviator glasses and gazed at me with eyes as blue as the Arctic Sea.

'What Khaled?' I asked.

'The night?'

'What? I no understand.'

I walked away. The man drove after me, keeping to my pace and tailing me until I reached the hostel. I turned around at the front door and saw him parking his car.

Quickly I ran up to our floor and searched for Khaled's mobile number. As soon as I'd found it, I went over to see the H&M Gang and strode into their room without knocking. Only Hewe was there. He was striking various poses in front of the mirror and admiring himself.

'Hey, what's up?'

'I need to use your mobile!'

'Why?'

'Khaled has fucked up! Please!'

I held up the piece of paper with the number on it. Hewe dialled it and passed me the phone.

'Don't break it or I'll kill you! And don't spend too long on it, either—I'm not Caritas!'

Holding the telephone to my ear, I walked back over to my room and threw myself angrily on the sofa.

'Yes?' said Khaled's voice at last.

'Hey, it's me, Karim from Niederhofen. There's a man here following me. He says he paid you.'

'A man in a Ferrari?'

'Yes.'

'That's Wolfram Maria von Richthausen. Everybody knows him. He's filthy rich.'

'I couldn't give a damn. What does he want from me?'

'I'm really sorry, Karim, but I needed the money. He saw you in the street and he's fancied you ever since. I sold you to him. For a hundred marks. Sorry, but I'd pimp the whole hostel for a hundred marks.'

'I'm going to kill you, Khaled.'

Richthausen followed me around Niederhofen for nearly six weeks. He would suddenly appear wherever I was in town, drive alongside me for a few yards, call out something and beckon to me. I was scared of him. On the one hand, I was stronger than him and could easily have dragged him from his car and beaten him up. On the other, I couldn't do anything because the man was clearly very powerful and I was just an asylum seeker. I endured his stalking and paid no attention to him. Then, virtually overnight, he left me alone.

The next time I saw him, *Frau* Schulz, was four months ago. There was a photo of him and his famous cat on the front page of a newspaper, and a picture of Khaled next to it. I stared at the headline in total shock: 'Iraqi admits Richthausen's murder.'

I skimmed through the short article. They had apparently got into an argument over sexual services rendered but unpaid. Khaled had flown off the handle and stabbed Richthausen with a kitchen knife.

I was amazed that fun-loving Khaled was capable of such an act. Over the following days there was wall-to-wall newspaper and TV coverage of him and his horrific crime. You must have heard about it too, *Frau* Schulz. After all, you knew Khaled.

Some of us sold their cocks and arses to earn a little dough on the side. Others became thieves or drug dealers. The rest of us, including me, had to survive on eighty marks per month.

There was only one legal means of topping up this amount. You gave us a hand, *Frau* Schulz. As asylum seekers we were not allowed to do a normal job, but your administration allowed us to do a so-called integration job for an hourly wage of one mark. No more than eighty hours per month, hence an extra eighty marks.

These 'integration jobs' often involved cleaning buildings or doing small gardening chores. Most asylum seekers, however, had no interest in these job offers. To be honest, I only did them for two reasons: because I was dying of boredom as I waited for the results of my asylum application, and because the money I earned was enough to buy myself a couple of cartons of cigarettes.

I was sick of scrounging cigarettes from passers-by in the street or filching ashtrays outside shops and pubs for fag butts to take a couple of puffs on.

Don't imagine for a moment, though, that begging for cigarettes is easy. It's an art you have to learn. It was the homeless Moroccan, Mohammed, who taught me the tricks of the trade, for he was a master in this field. You can't ask just anyone for a ciggy. You have to select a particular type of person —a man out walking with his wife and children, for example. He can't say no. How would he explain to his children that he'd failed to help a man in need? We hunted for these people and other suitable candidates in the pedestrian zone and along the riverside.

In my third week in Niederhofen, I went to the foreigners' registration office to see you, *Frau* Schulz, so I wouldn't have to practise this laborious craft any longer. You should have seen your face when I told you I'd come to volunteer for work. That permanently disgruntled expression vanished from your features, and for once you even gave me a friendly smile. That was the first and last time you've ever smiled at me. I imagine your face muscles ached afterwards: you probably hadn't used them for years.

'A job has just come up,' you said. 'For a refuse sorter. One of your people got his residence permit and doesn't need to rely on this work any more. You can take over his job. The tips are good. People are generous.'

The recycling centre was on the edge of town. It was a big space, fenced off with metal sheeting. There were a large number of different skips. In the middle of the plot was a Portakabin for the workers to take their breaks. There were also a small kitchen and a loo. It was hard communicating in Bavarian with the four nice employees, but they were used to working with guys like me. They were all around fifty years old—three women and *Herr* Bernhard. He taught me how to handle everything. I sorted waste, paper and other materials into the different skips. Overall, the work didn't require a vast amount of knowledge. I only had to learn a few words and phrases, which I used over and over again. Where does this go? Plastics or residual waste? Thank you. Please. Hello. Goodbye.

I constructed my sentences from these building blocks. I recycled and sorted words the same way I did rubbish.

The waste was as meticulously arranged as products in a well-stocked German supermarket: paper, organic waste, plastics, glass, construction waste, electrical waste, clothes, shoes and so on. Yet it still pained me to see all the things people threw away. At least half the rubbish would have been useful in an asylum seeker's hostel, even if most of it would have needed a little mending.

Another of my tasks was to assist the people who brought their stuff to the recycling centre. I took their bags and boxes from them and put the things in the right skips. It was true that the customers were generous: I often received fifty pfennig or one mark as a reward for my friendly manner. Some days I went home with an extra five to seven marks in my pocket.

One time I even got twenty marks. That was from Wolfram Maria von Richthausen, while he was still alive and following me to work, in the company of his aristocratic cat. He handed me a box containing two shirts in mint condition and a pair of shoes. I emptied it, upon which he slipped me a twenty-mark note, looked deep into my eyes as if intent on flirting with me and then walked away with his cat nestling in the crook of his elbow.

Working at the recycling centre was an absolute dream job. Every day I received some tips to finance my smoking habit. In addition, if only *Herr* Bernhard was there and I contrived to do it relatively inconspicuously, I was allowed to take whatever I wanted home with me. In the first month I got hold of a cassette recorder for our room, and I hauled a small TV halfway through Niederhofen to Ali and Salim's hostel.

Some of the other refugees in my hostel were quite envious of me. They noticed that I was now fairly well dressed compared to them. Of course I still couldn't sit down in the cafe or the pub every day like the locals, the gangsters or the toy boys, but I did allow myself this pleasure about once a week. Once, I was standing outside a snack bar eating a large durum doner kebab, when Sargon from the H&M Gang walked past and said something that made me feel quite proud: 'You've become very classy for a refuse sorter, eating one of those expensive durum wraps rather than a normal doner.'

I worked five hours per day from Monday to Thursday and met a lot of people who came to dispose of their rubbish. Very few young people, mainly elderly ladies and gentlemen. I was free for the rest of the week and would go on walks with the lads or stay at the hostel and dream of the reply from Nuremberg.

Summer came—my first summer in Germany. The sun now shone more frequently, and we were able to do lots of things outdoors. The first tourists appeared and wandered around the old town. Youngsters gathered on the riverbanks with their beer bottles, and the girls' laughter grew louder.

My days passed with the same steady sluggishness, though. I waited and waited. Then it was August, and everything changed overnight.

One morning *Herr* Bernhard told me that he had a new colleague on a permanent contract, which meant that my job ended that day. Utterly crestfallen, I took the bus back to the town centre and went straight to the foreigners' registration office. One of your colleagues, *Frau* Schulz, told me that he would look for a new job for me. That was two years ago, and I haven't heard from him to this day. You know what, though? Two weeks later I didn't have to do jobs like that any more because my right to asylum was finally recognized.

Salim was the first of us to receive a positive answer to his asylum application. We celebrated. Salim cooked Spanish tapas, and we chatted and drank until daybreak. We all dreamt of the day when we too might experience such a joyous moment to share with the others.

One week later Azrael brought me the green letter for which I'd been waiting for so long. I wavered over whether to open and read it, laid it on the table and stared at the envelope for several minutes, nibbling my lower lip until it was raw. Rafid grew impatient, then carefully opened it and flung his arms around me.

'Congratulations, my friend!'

It was pure chance and my greatest stroke of luck that my notification was sent before 9/11, for after the terrorist attacks on the World Trade Center and the Pentagon, no further notifications, either positive or negative, arrived at the hostel. It was as if the judges in Nuremberg had simply put the whole asylum procedure on ice because every refugee now came under general suspicion.

I took the letter to the foreigners' registration office. I was granted a two-year residence permit and received a blue passport of the kind issued to stateless people and those granted asylum. I could use the travel document to visit any country on earth—with the exception of Iraq of course. I looked forward to my life as a free man who could move around to his heart's content for two years. It was as if I'd been released after many years in prison.

Salim decided to travel directly to Munich and look for a job. His brother Majed lived there and could help him to find a place to stay in an expensive city, for starters. I, however, had no family outside Iraq. The only person I knew was Uncle Murad, my father's friend in Paris, but I couldn't afford to go anywhere outside Bavaria, and I wasn't authorized to work in France anyway. So I stayed in Niederhofen.

I now had one month to leave the asylum seekers' hostel and in that time I intended to get a job, health insurance and, above all, accommodation. Finding a flat was far from easy, however.

I went to see *Frau* Mohmadi from Caritas to ask her what I should do next. *Frau* Mohmadi in turn advised me to go to the job centre. *Herr* Sepp at the job centre then recommended that I should temp somewhere. Rafid had come along specially to act as my interpreter.

'I'd like to learn the language first, and to do that I need your help.'

'No problem. We're delighted that you want to learn our language,' said *Herr* Sepp, 'but first you have to work and pay taxes for a year, and then we can fund a language course for you.'

'But how am I supposed to work for a year, or even find a job in the first place, without knowing the language?'

'Like all your hard-working fellow Iraqis. I could arrange a job for you at Burger King. It's only a part-time job, but it's just the thing to get you started. You'll have health insurance, earn a little money and gradually be able to become a good *Bürger*.'

'I'm sorry,' said Rafid. 'What do you mean, "become a burger"?'

'Not burger,' said *Herr* Sepp. '*Bürger*. A citizen. A resident of this country. *Bürger*, with an umlaut. A German citizen. A German. At Burger King. Work. Then. *Bürger*.'

'Oh, I get it. I'm sorry.'

'Just come back to see us in a year,' *Herr* Sepp continued, 'and we'll take care of the language. If you don't want to work yet, that's fine too, but then you have to look after yourself. If you choose that option, we're not responsible for you—the social services is.'

'I'd rather have a different job, if that was at all possible.'

'Did you have a job back home?'

'Well, I was still at school. I did my final exams and then I ran away.'

'I'll see what I can do and then get back in touch with you.'

He pressed another slip of paper into my hand, telling me to present it at the social services office.

Rafid laughed himself hoarse on the way there, repeating the same phrase over and over again.

'A good *Bürger* at Burger King!'

A guy of about thirty called Krämer was in charge of my case at the social services office. He was as pale as a ghost. I imagine he was on serious medication and not in the best of health. He also seemed to have a slight disability and couldn't move his left hand properly. He didn't smile, but he didn't glare at me or seem irritated either; he was completely impassive, never betraying the slightest trace of emotion. He carried out his work with painful meticulousness, rigorously noting down everything I said. He listened closely, but showed not even the smallest reaction. He asked me to fill out several forms. I took them home with me and struggled for days to understand the many paragraphs and swathes of small print. Even Rafid was exasperated by the forms.

'I don't understand what it says, Karim, I really don't. It isn't German; it's Indonesian. We need a hand here. Maybe Katharina can help us?'

Katharina was a student who volunteered for Caritas, assisting *Frau* Mohmadi. Rafid, she and I spent around four hours filling out the forms. She wrote down anything she didn't understand and put the questions to *Herr* Krämer at the social services office over the phone. Finally, I signed all the paperwork and took it back to *Herr* Krämer, upon which he allocated me a room at the homeless hostel and a living allowance—three hundred and eighty marks per month, nonetheless. All of this was meant to tide me over until I found a job and a flat of my own.

On the day I received the money from social services, I bought myself a mobile phone with a prepaid card, immediately called my family in Baghdad and claimed I had already found a good job, rented a nice apartment in the centre of Niederhofen, was in good hands, and would very soon start my studies. Then my credit ran out, and we were cut off in mid-conversation.

In my naivety and enthusiasm I took *Herr* Krämer at his word when he said that this was an interim solution. I was convinced that it would be possible to find a proper job and even begin studying as soon as I'd learnt German. But that was a major delusion.

That was because my Iraqi high-school diploma wasn't recognized. I was told that I would have to attend a college for a year and sit the equivalent German exams before I'd be allowed to study. To get into that college I had to sit a different exam, and to be allowed to sit that exam I needed a language certificate—the general intermediate certificate from the Goethe Institute, which involved courses for language levels A1 to B2 along with extra preparatory courses for the test at the Goethe Institute itself or at another language school. Preparing for the entrance exam would therefore take at least twelve months and cost a fortune. Otherwise, I would have to work for twelve months in order for the job centre to fund my language course. I could therefore have begun to study, at the earliest, three years after my Iraqi high-school diploma had been recognized. That sure put paid to my enthusiasm.

The homeless hostel was out in the sticks. It took twenty-five minutes by bus to get to the centre of Niederhofen. The house must have been a hotel once. It had four floors, with rows of single rooms on each. The toilets and bathrooms were located at the beginning of each corridor. Many of the homeless people were either foreigners with a stay of deportation or German drug addicts. People like me stayed there for as short a time as possible until we'd found another flat.

There were constant bust-ups in this hostel too. The homeless Germans would hang around all day outside the hostel, swigging from beer bottles, fighting and shouting at each other. Then they would all sit down again and continue to talk, as if nothing had happened, slurring their words.

The only Niederhofeners who ventured to the homeless hostel were Jehovah's Witnesses. They even proselytized there. On only my second day they knocked on my door. I opened it. An elderly woman with a blissful smile on her face asked me if I believed in God.

'Sorry, what did you say?'

'Are you Muslim?'

'Yes. Why?'

'We help people to find their way to God.'

'I no understand German!'

'Never mind. Arabic?'

'Yes.'

She held out a brochure entitled 'Life'.

'Hayat?' My eyes glazed over, and I slammed the door.

When I'd taken a nap and managed to pull myself together again, I went over to see my neighbour Marco, a thirty-year-old Ethiopian who had been living in the hostel for three years and was quite muddleheaded. He told me that he'd been attending a kind of training course with the Jehovah's Witnesses for the past year.

'Every week, two women come to teach me. It's great. It's a free language lesson. I enjoy talking with women. I'm a homeless black African. What other woman so much as glances at me? It's only religious women who live for God who visit me here; no other woman even deigns to look at me.'

My neighbour on the other side, *Frau* Schulz, was Mohammed the Moroccan, the man who taught me how to cadge cigarettes. He too met the Jehovah's Witnesses every week. He claimed that Allah had given him an important task to fulfil with these women: to try to win them over to Islam during their weekly meetings.

Within a few days of arriving at the homeless hostel it was clear that I had to get out of there again as quickly as I could. I didn't want to end up like Marco and Mohammed. I tried my best, *Frau* Schulz, going to the job centre every day to look for a job. I was even willing to be a good *Bürger* or burger at Burger King, but then 9/11 happened, and it was impossible to get a job, even in a fast-food joint.

I clearly remember that day. I was lying in bed, just emerging from my midday nap. I was staring at the ceiling, savouring a wake-up cigarette, when someone suddenly started pounding on my door.

'Wake up, you lazy git!' It was Rafid's voice.

I leapt out of bed and opened the door. He shoved me out of the way without a word of greeting. His voice cracked. 'Revolution's broken out in America!'

'What's going on? Have you been smoking dope?'

'Oh come on, man. Turn the bloody TV on. Where's the remote?' I dug it out from under my bed sheets and turned on the TV. Wordlessly, Rafid pointed to the pictures.

'What's happening?' I asked him because I didn't understand what the newsreader was saying.

No one yet knew whether it was a military coup, an accident or a terrorist attack. Pure speculation. The reporter who kept appearing on screen looked as bewildered as we were.

'Are those scheduled airliners with passengers on board?'

'Don't think so,' said Rafid, without looking at me. 'Maybe a few American freedom fighters. Do you know what towers those are?'

'Nuh. Maybe they're something to do with the CIA.'

We had been through a lot, *Frau* Schulz, but neither of us had a clue about world affairs. We couldn't possibly have known it then, but that terrorist attack was to have a greater impact on our lives than any other prior event.

'I'm happy for the Americans,' said Rafid after a while.

'Huh?'

'At long last, they can see what it's like.'

My dear *Frau* Schulz, I too felt a vague sense of satisfaction at first. I couldn't ward it off: it just came over me all of a sudden. This was hardly surprising for an Iraqi. All I had known of Americans since childhood had been their fighter jets, their bombs and their missiles. They never brought anything else to my homeland.

Yet, as it gradually dawned on me during the day that the two towers didn't belong to the CIA, that no soldiers or spies had worked in those office blocks and that the aeroplanes had been carrying regular passengers, I fell into a bottomless pit of melancholia. *Frau* Schulz, I swear that I was ashamed of my initial schadenfreude. I'm still ashamed to this day.

From that accursed day onwards, the main term used to describe us Arabs in Germany was 'suspicious'. I would never have thought that terrorists hiding in Afghanistan's Hindu Kush mountains could, by their attacks in the United States, plunge my life in the Bavarian town of Niederhofen into such disarray. That's what you call globalization.

Before the end of September I received a letter from the police. It was a summons to an interview, and I was to bring it with me. The conversation took place at the criminal investigations branch of Niederhofen police station.

I was let in as soon as I arrived and showed the summons. A policeman escorted me to a small room and shut the door. I was alone. I thought I'd never make it out of there in one piece. The thing that really worried me, though, *Frau* Schulz, was the idea that I'd probably have to undress completely in front of the cops again. Once more they would grin, I thought, at the sight of my breasts, and once more one of them would stick his smelly finger up my arse—but this time he'd be looking for Osama bin Laden. At the same time, these concerns stuck me as trivial. The world was going berserk. It was the start of an international war on terror that would suck everyone into it, whether they liked it or not. And me? I was standing in Niederhofen police station. I didn't know why, but those damn breasts of mine occupied all my thoughts.

After a few minutes, three men in plain clothes entered the room. One of them was an interpreter, and I quickly identified his Lebanese roots from his dialect. He was wearing a gold cross around his neck and was therefore definitely a Christian. A man with a beard and a ruddy forehead introduced himself without shaking my hand.

'Dr Wurm, regional criminal investigations department.'

The third man was bald and wearing a black suit. He merely nodded and fiddled with a pen without saying a word. When I told Rafid about him later, he was convinced that the guy must be a member of the intelligence services.

Dr Wurm asked me to give honest answers. I wasn't suspected of anything, and this interview was a routine matter. The three men laid notebooks and pens out on the table. Dr Wurm also opened a blue folder and began by asking me for my name and profession, and about my parents, my siblings and my life in Iraq. In fact they were the same questions as at the hearing in Bayreuth when I'd applied for asylum. After a while, though, the questioning turned to religion.

'Are you Sunni?'

'No, I come from a Shiite family, but I'm not religious myself.'

'Shiite?'

'Yes.'

'Do you have any contacts with al-Qaida?'

'Sorry?'

'Do you have any contacts with al-Qaida?'

'I told you: I'm a Shiite. Al-Qaida is a Sunni organization. They kill Shiites because they regard them as corrupt Muslims. Do you really think I'd be in contact with people who want to murder my family and me?'

'Please answer my question. Do you have any contacts with al-Qaida?'

'No.'

'Do you know anyone who works with al-Qaida or has sympathy for the organization?'

'No.'

'Are you a terrorist?'

I was silent for a little too long.

'Please answer my question. Are you a terrorist?'

'For hell's sake, no!'

'Have you carried out any bomb attacks?'

'No, no.'

'Do you intend to carry out attacks or become a terrorist?'

'No, no, no.'

'Are you willing to work with the German state?'

'I'm a polite person and I will gladly help you, but I won't work as a spy.'

At some point the bald man, who so far hadn't said a word, handed me a list of forty-four organizations and parties classified as terrorist from around the world; it even included the Red Army Faction. I had to mark on the list whether I approved of these organizations or was in contact with them, ticking either 'Yes' or 'No'. Forty-four times I ticked 'No', then they let me go.

The others were summoned to this kind of interview too. I was very cautious for the next few months because I was worried that I was under surveillance. I never voiced any opinions on political and religious subjects over the phone, let alone anything to do with 9/11. I never criticized Americans, Europeans or Germans. I rarely talked about Arab dictators because some of them were American allies.

It was a thrilling time to be alive, *Frau* Schulz. Don't you agree? Everyone was freaking out. Some of us did actually make deals with the state and provide intelligence on other refugees. The three H&M Gang members must have entered into some kind of agreement because all three of them suddenly received residence permits, although they'd been waiting for the results of their asylum applications for years and should have been rejected due to their criminal records.

I was invited a second time to the police station. It was shortly after the Americans had marched into my homeland, Iraq. I was asked exactly the same questions all over again.

People were suspicious and fearful of anything foreign. East and West, Orient and Occident, Osama and Bush. We all had far too many headlines and opinions swirling around in our heads like will-o'-the-wisps. The displays in bookshops around town changed, with Islam and terrorism dominating the shelves. There were suddenly books with titles like *Prophets of Terror*, *Aisha: I Was the Imam's Seventeenth Wife* and *The Ex-Terrorist*.

German TV was now filled with Arabs and migrants, explaining in fluent German how evil and dangerous Islam could be. In all my time in Germany I'd never seen any in the media before, and now they were everywhere, on special reports and talk shows. Their German current accounts swelled at the same rate as the mountains of corpses in their native countries. We called them 'vampire intellectuals'.

The world was going berserk. People were going berserk. It wasn't just we Arabs and Muslims under suspicion; entire neighbourhoods were cordoned off every time a suitcase was left somewhere. Battle-hardened specialists had to be called to remove them. Every piece of luggage in the world and every other rubbish bag was suddenly suspect.

This lunacy drove some of us to become fanatics. Yes, *Frau* Schulz, now the bad Muslims did indeed turn bad.

The first person to catch the bug was Dumpster Ali. In the space of a few weeks he morphed from a kindly man into a fundamentalist. He'd always been devout, but he'd never had a problem with people like Rafid and me. Quite the opposite: he had considered us his family in Germany. However, at Christmas of all times, everything came to a head.

Rafid had invited Ali and me over to the hostel for Christmas Eve and was planning to cook us dinner. 'We don't give a damn about Christmas,' he said, 'but we might as well celebrate if everyone else is.'

I was looking forward to an evening in my old haunts and brought along a few cans of beer. When I cracked open the second can, Ali could no longer take it. 'I don't agree with what you're doing.'

'What do you mean?'

'You always do their bidding. You're only drinking beer so they'll leave you in peace.'

'What? Who?'

'The Christians. The Germans.' An ancient fire suddenly smouldered in Ali's eyes. 'Why are you selling out your culture to people who despise you?'

'What culture?' asked Rafid.

'Our culture as Muslims. They're abusing us here. They present our religion as something bestial. And you just let them do it? You even go along with them?'

'Are you making fun of us, Ali?' asked Rafid.

'No, *you* are making fun of our culture, and I'm defending it.'

'I drink beer because it tastes good, not to pretend I'm German,' I said.

Rafid now got extremely wound up and angry. 'Ali, you can't even read or write! What do you know about religion and culture? What the hell are you talking about?' Boiling with fury, he banged the saucepan against the wall. The tomato sauce, complete with pieces of meat, spilt out of the pot onto the kitchen floor. Ali got up and left the room without a word.

How could it have come to this? So our Ali was now a radical Muslim, ranting about everything. Rafid was open-minded and cosmopolitan, and he too was ranting about everything. He went on rants about Americans, Arabs, Muslims, Christians and even me. What about me? I made myself comfortable. I let Rafid spout on angrily, drank cans of beer, ate peanuts, kept my mouth shut and watched *Home Alone*.

A few days later, Ali asked to see us again. He apologized for his weird behaviour and drank black tea with us, but otherwise he said little and then left.

'That was the last we'll see of him,' Rafid commented after he'd gone.

'What makes you say that?'

'Just a hunch. We've lost him.'

Where he was wrong was about never seeing Ali again. Where he was right was that our relationship with Ali would never be the same again.

Ali had befriended two men in his hostel, and from then on they whiled away their time together. They were Iraqis like us, but someone seemed to have bashed them all over the head with the Koran. These three religious boneheads hung out together at the hostel.

Rafid and I knew a lot of people but we never succeeded in making any new friends in Niederhofen. All our ties in the homeless hostel and both asylum seekers' hostels were always very loose. Four of us had come here from Bayreuth, but now there were only two of us left: Salim had moved to Munich, and

Ali had become a super-Muslim. So just two of us celebrated our first New Year's Eve in Germany.

Carrying a few beers and a bottle of vodka, we strolled down the street from the station and then from the town square through the pedestrian zone towards the riverbank. Rafid and I had drunk everything by the time we got there. We could barely speak, but we were desperate to get hold of one last bottle of beer so that we could smash it on the asphalt on the stroke of midnight. For some reason we thought, in our alcoholic fog, that this would make a fitting ending to the year.

Unfortunately, however, all the grocery stores and supermarkets had already closed; there wasn't a single open shop in sight. The riverside bars and pubs were indeed full of drunken Niederhofeners, but a beer cost three times more there than in a supermarket. So we kept walking in the hope that we might find something somewhere.

When we reached the bridge, Rafid suddenly thought of a filling station as a last resort. They were open round the clock, and so we sought out somebody to tell us where we might find the nearest one. By this time it was quarter to twelve.

Rafid was so drunk that he lost all inhibitions and went over to a blonde girl sitting on a wall on her own with a bottle of sparkling wine by her side.

'Beautiful lady! Where is the nearest filling station?'

'What do you want with a filling station at this time?' She smiled. A good sign.

'I want to buy some alcohol!'

'Well, you won't find one around here. The nearest filling station's half an hour's walk away. You won't make it there before twelve.'

'So what should I do?' slurred Rafid.

The evening went the way it was destined to go from here. Rafid and the young woman flirted with each other. Her name was Annika, and at midnight we stood on the bridge with her and drank her sparkling wine. A few hours later Rafid went home with Annika, and I returned to my hostel alone.

The next day, Rafid came over to tell me all about it. 'When I woke up this morning, she was lying next to me in bed, her body gleaming, the colour of milk. I briefly thought about waking her up, but then I decided to get a rose for her first. I searched for her front-door key and found it in the lock. I took it with me and left the flat. The streets were empty, and all the shops were closed. I looked around and spotted a small old cemetery. I went in, stole a red rose from somewhere, thanked the grave's owner and hurried back to Annika's flat.'

Rafid's tale was full of romantic details. Rafid had really fallen for Annika, with her blue eyes and her Bavarian hips. He didn't leave her side for two weeks, and he was in seventh heaven. Then, however, she had to return to London; she was studying something or other at King's College. She did keep in touch with Rafid for some time, but after a while she stopped giving any signs of life. The whole situation had probably got to her: Rafid had no money and he wasn't allowed to work or travel.

All of this hit my friend pretty hard. For weeks he refused to see anyone in his disappointment in life. It was during this period that Rafid began to write.

While this was going on, I kept looking for a job. I rang Salim in Munich in utter desperation to ask for his advice.

'A temping agency should be able to help you out.'

'What's that?'

'A firm that finds work for you. You sign a contract with them, and then they look for a job for you. They lease you to other companies when those companies need short-term staff. Of course, the temping agency takes a cut from your wages, but then again they provide you with more jobs.'

That same day I rang my case handler at the job centre and arranged an appointment with him. He gave me three addresses in Niederhofen and told me to go directly to see them. In late January I signed a contract with one of those temping agencies. It was called Hoffmann & Sons. I would earn four and a half euros per hour.

Yep, that too had changed over the New Year. The deutschmark had been abolished and an official exchange rate of one euro for 1.95583 marks was set. At a stroke everything became more expensive. I would never have been able to keep my head above water if it hadn't been for Hoffmann & Sons. Within a few days I did indeed get my first job.

The ironworks were in a village just outside Niederhofen called Neuhofen. My job was to saw up iron. I stood by a huge machine and waited for other workers to bring me the iron plates. These I fed into a machine, pressed a green button and the thing made loads of noise. I had to wear yellow ear-protectors at all times.

Many of my colleagues were heavily built men whose German I couldn't understand because they spoke an impenetrable Bavarian dialect. The rest were foreigners, mostly Eastern Europeans, and they had their own cliques. I found it difficult to communicate with the others due to my poor vocabulary. I worked in that factory for almost four months, returning exhausted to the homeless hostel every evening and slumping down in front of the TV until I dozed off.

When my spell at the ironworks came to an end, I was eager to leave the hostel, so I looked for a flat. Every Saturday morning I went to the editorial offices of the local newspaper, which had display cases outside containing that day's edition. I jotted down the relevant phone numbers from the rental adverts.

Everyone I rang asked where I came from and then either hung up or hummed and hawed. It was seven weeks before a lady let me visit an apartment. I took that tiny one-room flat, even though it was very expensive for me—three hundred and sixty euros, heating included. It lay in the middle of the industrial estate between a DIY superstore and a hypermarket.

Hoffmann & Sons sent me to a new workplace, a shampoo factory this time. My task couldn't have been any easier. I stood at a conveyor belt and had to adjust the position of any bottles that weren't standing correctly on the belt so that the advancing machine could pop lids on them. I performed the same movement every day, like a robot. Staring for hours at an endless line of identical shampoo bottles made me tired and affected my concentration.

My companions on the conveyor belt were two women, a young Iranian called Elham and Hilde, a German of around fifty. Week after week, Hilde complained about her husband, who apparently cheated on her, regularly beat her and spent all her money. The Iranian woman completely ignored me and barely spoke a word to me.

I stayed at that factory for nine weeks until the employee I'd replaced while he was on sick leave came back, and I had to leave, for those were the rules.

I was able to stay longer at my next workplace. For six months I worked for a cleaning firm called Cleanteam 2000. My boss was a Palestinian. From the very first day it was clear that, despite sharing the same language, we were not going to get along. He wore a watch with a colour photo of Saddam Hussein on the dial and constantly got on my nerves.

'Saddam is the only real man in Iraq,' he would say. 'You Iraqis don't deserve such a great man as your leader. You run off abroad and leave him to fight alone!'

Luckily, my boss and I rarely crossed each other's path. He would occasionally check our work and then vanish again.

I was given three addresses to clean every day. I was fully responsible for the first: from one to four in the afternoon I cleaned the corridors of a private clinic that was practically always empty. Afterwards I went to the local newspaper's offices, where I cleaned from five to eight alongside a sixty-year-old Bulgarian woman called Ioana. One floor of the same building belonged to Allianz Insurance, and we cleaned there from nine to eleven in the night. Ioana was kind and helpful, but she didn't speak any German. Her vocabulary consisted of a few fragments, such as 'yes', 'no', 'thanks', 'please', 'bye', 'clean', 'don't clean', so we never chatted much.

At the end of my last day of work for Cleanteam 2000, I went up to my boss and said, 'I'm going to go to the mosque soon and pray that Allah sends you Palestinians a leader like Saddam!' before spitting on the floor by his feet.

I had the feeling, dear *Frau* Schulz, that I was getting dumber by the day. I worked incessantly, got home fatigued, ate toast with margarine and ketchup, watched telly and went to bed. Only at weekends did I occasionally go out with Rafid.

What's more, I hadn't saved a single cent towards my operation and had sent no money to my family, who were desperate for my help. My meagre wages didn't allow me to do either of those things.

However, I wanted to do everything possible to ensure that I worked for a full year because only then would the job centre be willing to fund my language course. I kept hearing *Herr* Sepp's words echoing in my ears: 'We're delighted that you want to learn our language, but first you have to work and pay taxes for a year, and after that we can fund a language course for you.'

I stuck to my task and completed my year in February 2003. I terminated my contract with Hoffmann & Sons and went to the job centre. After two years in Germany I could actually attend a German course at last.

You can certainly take some pride in me, *Frau* Schulz. Not everyone makes it as I did.

Frau Schulz, please excuse me for a moment. I just have to see if Lada has finally got in touch. Stupid cow, she knows I'm leaving the country today, and yet it doesn't even occur to her to ring me or send me a bloody text at least.

Oh, Lada had me at her mercy. I'd fallen head over heels in love with her.

The first time I really noticed her was in Lidl. I was standing near the snacks, staring at the pistachios, when she suddenly said something beside me.

'You in German lesson, yes?'

And there she was, Lada, standing there, holding her two-year-old daughter's hand.

Lada is amazingly beautiful. She's a little taller than me and very slim, and she has short blonde hair, dark-brown eyes and shimmering white skin, as if she's just stepped out of an advert for a night cream.

'Yes.'

'Me too. You coming tomorrow? Lesson?'

'Yes. Great.'

'Great.'

'Great.'

'See you tomorrow.'

'See you tomorrow.'

The next morning Lada walked straight over to my desk in the classroom, kissed me on the cheek and sat down beside me. I've been infatuated with her ever since.

Lada comes from the former Soviet Union, she grew up somewhere in the Belarusian countryside. Her father drove an old Lada truck, which he loved more than anything else, so he went and named his daughter after it. She'd never really considered moving to Germany or elsewhere in Europe, but the crises and riots in her homeland preyed on her and her husband Dimitri's minds. They sought a way out—and they found one. They saved up for a long time until a civil servant, in return for two months' wages, issued them a document confirming Lada's Jewish origins. They'd heard that people of Jewish heritage could be immediately granted German residence permit as quota refugees. Lada would claim henceforth that her grandparents had emigrated from Nazi Germany to Russia and remained there until their deaths. She'd never met them and she hadn't been brought up as a Jew, but as a Christian.

It took a long time for all the formalities to be taken care of and for notification to arrive from the embassy. Ever since she had been considered a German Jew. Dimitri was also granted a residence permit as her husband, even though he too was born a Christian.

She once told me that many people from the former Soviet Union had faked their papers to be able to live in Germany. Christian and Muslims from the USSR invented German ancestors. Certain civil servants and police officers in their homeland had turned this into a flourishing business. Anyone able to pay could officially become a Jew and receive state confirmation of that fact. These certificates cost between two thousand and ten thousand dollars, depending on the amount of work involved. Jews used to have to conceal their identity to survive, whereas nowadays people will pay good money to become Jewish. The world's a strange place, *Frau* Schulz, don't you agree?

Lada doesn't have an easy life in Germany. She looks after her child, learns German in her spare time and also works twenty hours per week as a cleaner at Niederhofen district hospital—even though she receives an extra allowance for quota refugees. She has to provide for three people, though, as Dimitri spends the whole day lazing on the couch, guzzling beer and vodka.

Lada touched parts of my heart I didn't even know existed. It's like doing a new sport and feeling aches and pains in places where you've never felt any muscles before. I'd do anything to make Lada happy.

Lada was the strong character in our relationship, and I was the fool. I knew and sensed this from the very beginning, but I didn't care. I couldn't alter it. Our first kiss was beside the Danube. After our lesson, we'd been celebrating our teacher *Frau* Müllerschön's birthday along with the other students. Afterwards, Lada and I went for a walk along the river on our own and sat down on a bench. It was already getting dark, and the sky was gradually turning a pastel shade of pink. The river gurgled merrily against the bank beneath our feet. It was March, the first slightly warmer day of the year.

I asked Lada if everything was all right because she seemed so absent the whole time. She began to weep.

'Dimitri hit me yesterday.' She pushed up her T-shirt to show me some huge bruises on her back. 'With his belt. He accused me of being up to something with you, even though I've only mentioned you once or twice.'

I looked into her eyes and without thinking I kissed a blue spot on her collarbone. She sat still and appeared to like it. Then our lips met.

Frau Schulz, I don't quite know how to describe the relationship initiated by that kiss. It was all a blur. Dimitri was always at home when I went to see Lada—officially to learn English with her. Each visit began with my having to drink vodka and beer with him. However, the guy cannot really be said to have drunk: he was more like a human drain for alcohol. He would pour litres of vodka down his throat before falling into a snoring, drunken stupor on the couch. Dimitri wasn't particularly tall and he was very thin. Each time, I carried him to bed like a loving father would his child, closed the door on him and was then alone with Lada. She had usually just done the same with her daughter Maja, tucked her in and singing her a lullaby.

During the first three weeks, I visited her at home and she kept me hanging on, not yet ready to go to bed with me. To be honest, though, I didn't want to either at that time. I'd never slept with a woman, dear *Frau* Schultz. And in a way I'm half woman myself.

Despite how much I wanted to touch Lada, my breasts made me insecure and anxious, and so we simply snogged and stroked each other a bit at first. Of course she noticed my unpractised hands and my nervousness, so she led the way. I often intended to tell her I was still a virgin, but male pride wouldn't let me utter those words. I knew she knew, and I found that embarrassing enough. Except my breasts embarrassed me more. I always wore a skintight vest that kept them pressed flat when I went to her place, and I had to take enormous care whenever we touched each other. Once, when she tried to remove my shirt, I pushed her hands away a little too abruptly.

'What is it?' she asked.

'I don't want to talk about it.'

'Do you have scars? I guessed as much.'

'Yes.' I said nothing, thinking fast. 'I was tortured in prison. It looks horrible.'

'It's okay.'

'Thank you.'

I so wanted to tell her everything, about how I'd grown these damn breasts and how they'd turned my life upside down. But I couldn't do it, *Frau* Schulz. Yes, I'm ashamed of that, too. Twice over, in fact: once for my breasts, and second for making up a bad story to mask my own bad story. But to be honest I was also glad. After that, Lada never tried to take my shirt off again, making our love life much easier for me.

We first did it on a Friday evening. Dimitri drank himself unconscious as usual. This time he also poured Lada more vodka than normal and forced her to drink it after she'd put the kid to bed.

'I want to study later,' she said.

He laughed and as usual his slightly oversized golden incisor sparkled in his open mouth. He wouldn't take no for an answer, staring at Lada until she finally knocked back the vodka.

Around nine o'clock I carried Dimitri into the bedroom and pulled the covers over him. I don't really know why I took so much care of him, for actually I couldn't stand him. He was a good-for-nothing and a violent drunkard who regularly beat Lada, and for that I would gladly have smothered him with the pillow right there and then. Suddenly, however, he opened his bloodshot eyes and grabbed my wrist.

'I don't want a black child, all right?'

Before I could say anything, he turned on his side and started snoring again. I shut the door and went back into the living room. Lada was lying on the sofa. She'd hidden her head under a cushion and was mewing and hissing like a cat. I sat down beside her.

'Dimitri knows about us?'

'I think so.' Her head was still under the cushion, muffling her voice.

'I thought he would kill you if he found out.'

'He loves me, and I love him. He's my husband and the father of my child.'

'And what does that make me?' I pulled the cushion away from her face and stroked her short hair.

'You're drunk.'

'I'm being serious, Lada. What do I mean to you?' I noticed that I was getting angrier with every word.

'No idea. Leave me alone. If you're not happy, you can leave.' She pushed me away from her. 'You're a total weakling.'

Without warning I threw myself on top of her, put one hand around her throat and clenched my fingers. 'Stop messing with me. Do you understand?'

She writhed between my hands, trying to break free. I pushed her head down harder onto the cushion. She hit me in the face. I hit her in the face too. Her body bucked and she thrashed her legs about. I pressed her down onto the sofa with my entire weight, then hit her again. I noticed how she suddenly gave in and ceased fighting.

Then she carefully touched my face and laid one hand gently on my cheek. She stretched up to me with her lips, and we kissed urgently.

I pushed up her dress. Like a wild animal, I tore her knickers apart. I was more aroused than I'd ever been in my entire life. Thousands of emotions merged and raged inside me, *Frau* Schulz. I grabbed hold of Lada and spun her around. I licked her from behind with one finger in her backside. Then I undid my trousers and spat on my penis before pushing it slowly into Lada's arse. I came before I'd even fully entered her. Then I wept. With shame, out of loneliness, with joy, with pride, from pain, from grief, out of love. I simply remained inside her, slapping her gently on the backside and weeping. In the meantime Lada pleasured herself, and when she'd come, we lay entwined on the sofa for a long time, stroking our wounds.

That night broke the knot in our relationship. We both felt liberated. I quickly learnt what she wanted in bed: she liked soft, tender foreplay with lots of fervent kissing and gentle stroking and cuddling, but when we got down to it, it had to be as hard as possible. That wasn't so easy for me because I otherwise played the submissive role in our relationship, but I gradually grew into my part.

Over time, I also found out how to keep it up for longer and not to come too early each time. I had to think of something completely unerotic to avoid premature ejaculation. So there were times when I was getting it on with Lada but thinking of Saddam Hussein. Or of you, *Frau* Schulz: it worked wonders.

Our relationship lasted for almost three months, the same length of time as our language course. Then everything changed.

As I was leaving Lada's house in the middle of the night for the umpteenth time, I had the impression that someone was tailing me in a car on my way to the bus stop. At first I didn't give it any further thought and took the next bus home to the industrial estate. There, the car was waiting again, just behind the bus shelter. I walked straight towards it.

Four men got out. I couldn't make out their faces in the dark, but they spoke Russian to one another. They ran towards me and shoved me to the ground, then beat me unconscious.

When I came to, I felt as if I'd been run over by a car. I hauled myself to my flat and went straight to the bathroom. I saw an unrecognizable face in the mirror—a swollen red-and-blue frog covered with blood and with an open cut under its right eye. It was painful as I washed my face, then I lay down in bed. Squinting as eyes swelled shut, I wrote a text to Lada.

'Friends of Dimitri's beat me up. What do we do now?'

She didn't answer. Instead, she was standing on my doorstep the next morning. 'Oh, shit!' she said when she saw my battered face. 'Are you okay? I mean, are you badly hurt?' She went to touch my face, but then held back to avoid causing me even more pain. 'Are you planning to go to the police?' Her tone suggested not that she thought this was a good idea but that she was scared of Dimitri.

'What would I tell the police? My girlfriend's husband sent people I can't describe to beat me up? Of course not. But the more important question is what *we're* going to do now?'

At once Lada's expression, voice and whole demeanour changed. She turned ice-cold. 'Listen, Karim. I don't want you to end up as a corpse. I'm not going to leave my husband: a child needs its father. Our relationship ends here. It's better for all of us. We had fun. And now I've got to go to work. Take care.'

Without looking around again, she disappeared down the stairs. I haven't seen her since. From time to time I sent her a message, but I never received an answer. Yesterday I wrote to tell her that I intend to emigrate to Finland now.

I miss her greatly. I miss everything about her: her lips, her smile, her kisses, her tears, her hardness. I shouldn't waste any more thought on Lada. A new woman awaits me in Finland, *Frau* Schulz. That much is certain.

I'm still lying on the sofa. I have no idea if I'm dreaming or just completely stoned.

Waves of pictures and memories break over me. Floods of people hurry past me and trip over one another. I'm a tree. I'm rooted in the ground. Everything's spinning. Places vanish, appear and move away again. I'm sitting by the window of a train. I'm hurtling through space. I'm hurtling through time.

A man sits down on the sofa. Dense fog obscures his face. Only gradually does it clear. I can't recognize anything. But I can smell it. He used to wear this aftershave every day. It's his aftershave. What's he doing here?

'Halim, my brother?' I say.

I can't hold back my tears. I haven't seen him in ages. Since he went to war. Oh, how I miss him! But now he's here. He's sitting there. He's alive.

I try to touch him. I want to hug him, but I can't move.

'I'm a tree, brother. I can't move. Come to me, please!'

Halim smiles, but then he slowly dissolves. I just about see the last part of him, his shoes, fly through the ceiling and disappear.

'Please stay, Halim!'

My parents are here too. My mother. All the world's emotions are gathered on her face. She looks so meek.

'Your brother died at the front, my son!'

'Mother? Is that you?'

Then I'm once more sitting by the window of the train. I'm hurtling through space. I'm hurtling through time. Everything rushes past.

I'm in my room in Baghdad. I see myself, as if I existed in duplicate. I watch myself, but I'm not in myself. I'm there and also not there. I can't talk to myself. Who's sitting there? He screams very loudly. Oh God, how it hurts my ears. I can't understand what he's saying. Which language is he speaking? I'm back in the train. I can't distinguish anything outside. I don't know where I am.

Then I see my father. We're walking through Munich together. He's insistently talking to me.

'Go and never come back! Only death is normal here.'

German police officers are chasing us. We run. When I look back to find him, he's gone.

I'm back in Salim's flat. I'm still lying on the sofa. Am I really stoned? I have to leave for Finland any minute. Where's Salim? I'm hungry.

'Salim?'

My German language course began about three weeks before the Americans invaded Iraq. I was highly motivated and wanted to do everything faultlessly, *Frau* Schulz. I'd bought myself a notebook, a few pencils, a rubber, a pencil sharpener and a black rucksack. Every morning I got up at seven o'clock, got ready and took the bus to school. I was a proper German schoolboy.

Except that the school building wasn't a real school building, but a large room in a converted barn on a farm to the north of town. Along with sixteen other pupils, most of them senior citizens who, like Lada, came from the former Soviet Union, I devoted myself henceforth for six hours every day to learning German personal pronouns, regular and irregular verbs, adjectives and prepositions. For the first twenty days, I was top of the class. I was a real swot and wanted to learn everything. After all, I'd waited two years for this course.

Soon, however, *Frau* Müllerschön started to call me a lazy git. It began when war broke out in my homeland. I no longer did my homework and my mind was usually elsewhere. Now and then, at the beginning, Lada forced me to study with her on her sofa, but I preferred to escape with her, diving into her body to forget the outside world.

It was extremely tough for me right then. It had been hard before the war, but now it was even harder, *Frau* Schulz. In recent months, the Americans had contacted all the Iraqi dissidents in exile, from communists through to the small Shiite and Kurdish parties, who sat down with them to discuss how to wage a war to topple Saddam and his regime. We'd even heard about it in Niederhofen.

I was a mess, worrying about my family in Baghdad and how they would get through another war. Even Rafid, whose stance on things was normally clear, was confused.

'We're in an absurd predicament. Either we continue to put up with a fucking dictatorship that destroys our souls, or we join the US and wage a fucking war that destroys our country. We're suddenly supposed to choose between shit and shit. I can't make up my mind, Karim, for fuck's sake.'

During that time I went to my very first demonstration. It was organized by students from Niederhofen University. Rafid and I marched with around seven hundred total strangers, hurling insults at the Americans. A few skinheads brought their German flags and shouted along with everyone else. On all sides there were riot police, armed to the teeth and watching our every step.

The refugees in Niederhofen argued violently with each other that day, even during the demonstration. Some marchers were in favour of the US plan and welcomed the invasion. One man described Bush as the true prophet of our times. He was even ready to beat Rafid up because Rafid couldn't get his head around the man's position.

'I'm against the dictatorship,' said Rafid, 'but I'm also against this war.'

'You're either with us or against us! We don't want to listen to your intellectual garbage!'

'Oh, piss off!'

Another asylum seeker reacted by spitting in Rafid's face. We left the demonstration and caught the bus back to my place in the industrial estate.

I switched on the TV and we watched the news. One programme that day had invited an Iraqi author who lived in Germany like us and wrote in German.

'It's highly likely that many Iraqis will lose their lives in this war,' he said, 'but even more will be able to lead a normal life after it when the dictatorship is gone. We're sacrificing a few so that the others can survive. We have no choice. If there's no meat, one is happy to eat tripe. We must cooperate with the Americans.'

'Almost every Iraqi in Niederhofen,' said Rafid, 'thinks like that author. Maybe every Iraqi in the whole world. But no one wants to imagine that their own families might be among the victims.'

I said nothing.

'We've got a real problem, Karim. We've been wallowing in the swamps of dictatorship, war and embargoes for so long that we've become helpless. It doesn't matter any more who helps us. It makes no difference if it's the Saudis or the Yankees. Most people just want to be rescued—and that's dangerous.'

The next day we went back on the streets to demonstrate. This time we tried to avoid the other refugees. Standing in front of the town hall with a few young students and punks, we shouted all kinds of slogans targeting both Saddam and Bush.

Yet the participants didn't get on at this demonstration either. An elderly woman wearing a Palestinian scarf stared at us peculiarly for a long time, as if we were aliens who'd landed on the wrong planet because we alternated Bush-bashing and Saddam-bashing. She came over to us.

'Are you Iraqis?'

'Yes.'

'What you're doing here brings shame on your country. Saddam is the only one who stands up to the imperialists.'

'He's a dictator,' I said.

'Where's your proof?'

'Sorry?'

'It's all capitalist propaganda!'

I spotted that Rafid was on the point of throttling the woman. I grabbed him by the shoulder and pushed him away slowly.

'Leave us alone!'

The first bombs fell on Baghdad on a Thursday. Fighter planes quickly destroyed all its bridges and the power station. They carried out attacks on every major military base and administrative building in the country. The war escalated with every passing day.

I spent every free minute I had watching the news and following the war. I could no longer get through to my parents by phone. I stared at the TV, hoping that the missiles didn't strike the areas where my relatives lived.

I lived in a capsule. I was neither optimistic nor pessimistic, feeling instead emotionally numb, constantly looking for something to distract myself. During the day I went to school, in the afternoons I watched the news, occasionally I drank vodka in the evenings with Dimitri and then had sex with his wife Lada. Around midnight I went home, watched more news, went to bed and so on, over and over again. A bomb fell there. Vodka was drunk here. A person died there. Knickers were pulled down here. A child was wounded there. I had an orgasm here. It was ludicrous. Everything took place simultaneously, and everything seemed to take place simultaneously inside me.

If for some reason I wasn't spending the evening at Lada's, I'd meet up with Rafid and we watched the news together. Rafid was pessimistic, claiming that this war spelt the end of any dreams in Iraq for the next four or five generations. He stopped telling jokes, became very serious, chain-smoked and was often silent.

The war was over sooner than we expected. After two and a half weeks, the large statue of Saddam Hussein in Baghdad's Firdoz Square came down. Here in Niederhofen, *Frau* Schulz, in my flat between the DIY superstore and the hypermarket, Rafid and I stood in my room together, gazing at the footage. We wept and embraced.

The war in Iraq was declared officially over in May, but in September a new war began for us in Germany. The authorities now began firing off one revocation missile after another at us Iraqi asylum seekers.

You, *Frau* Schulz, you sent mine.

Do you know, *Frau* Schulz, what Saddam Hussein called the First Gulf War in 1991? *Umm-al-Maarek*. That roughly translates as the 'mother of all battles'. After the capitulation, however, the Iraqi people sarcastically referred to the war as the 'mother of all defeats'.

The president named the second war in 2003 *Umm-al-Hawasim*—the 'mother of all decisive moments'. After Saddam Hussein's fall, the country's poor and thieves pillaged every administration, museum and bank. Ever since, the war has been popularly known as the 'mother of all robberies'.

If I were to describe my past year in Germany, *Frau* Schulz, I would call it the 'mother of all failures'. This year has been so awful that even our court jester Rafid has completely stopped telling any jokes. In August he was admitted to Mainkofen psychiatric hospital. Before winding up there, though, he got up to all kinds of crazy things. The hardcore medication has relaxed him a little now. He doesn't curse any more, barely moves, doesn't come up with any madcap ideas and causes less bother than he used to. One might say that his brain has gone into hibernation.

I always thought I knew him well and that we were best friends. Salim often referred to us as 'two buttocks in the same pair of underpants'—'neither of you exists without the other'. The truth, though, is that I only knew about his life in Germany. I know very little about his past.

Rafid was a secretive and peculiar character who knew every trick in the book. If his life had turned out differently, he would doubtless have become a famous, even legendary figure. But where would he have got that chance, *Frau* Schulz? Amid the chaos of the Iraq war, perhaps, or in Germany in its coffin of bureaucracy and fear?

I think that writing was the only reason he didn't go mad sooner. Even back in Bayreuth people called Rafid 'Pencil' because he always had one tucked behind his ear.

Somewhere in his writings one must be able to find the answer to the question of why he's now stuck in a madhouse. Unfortunately, none of us has ever been able to read those texts.

'I'll give you my novel when it's finished.' That's what Rafid said every time I asked him about it, but he never finished it. I presume that Rafid chucked all his notes into the rubbish bin—two whole boxes stuffed with them. We couldn't find them in his room, anyway.

It was incredibly difficult for him to write abroad. He possessed, for example, no historical and lexical tools in Arabic. He often asked the hostel's other residents about real-life events, names or dates, and was like a happy child when he obtained the information he was looking for.

Moreover, there were no bookshops in Niederhofen selling foreign-language books. We heard that such shops did exist in big cities such as Hamburg, Cologne and Berlin. He always longed to travel to one of those cities and go to those shops.

However, his asylum application was turned down about two years ago, like Dumpster Ali's. He'd been living in the homeless hostel on a stay of deportation ever since. Even if he had managed to find a way of getting hold of such reference books, he couldn't have afforded to buy one. A book like *The History of Iraq*, which he so desperately wanted, costs at least twenty-five euros, and there was no decent lending library in Niederhofen that stocked foreign books.

'If I assess my situation properly and then exaggerate it a little,' he once said, 'my writing is clearly a crime because I work for six to eight hours daily on my book. That's forbidden by law because I don't have a work permit. If I finish the book and it's published and sells well, I'll probably end up in jail. In the name of the law against illegal employment! Back home I was allowed to write as much as I wanted, but I had to censor myself if I didn't want to die. Here in democratic Germany, on the other hand, my very attempts to write are a crime!'

Yes, *Frau* Schulz, back then Rafid still had the sense of humour we all loved so much, and because he was so crafty, one day he discovered a source from which he could coax some information.

The bank branch in Niederhofen's pedestrian zone had a computer with an Internet connection in the lobby. It was in the middle of the room with the cash machines, and anyone could use it free of charge. Of course every boy, girl, homeless person, asylum seeker and foreigner in town wanted to try out the Internet, so it was completely impossible to get an hour to yourself on that computer.

One time Foad, a member of the H&M Gang, got into an argument with a girl about that machine. Foad didn't want to stop surfing, although the girl had been waiting for ages. He insulted her, the girl called her boyfriend who called his friends and it escalated into a brawl. The police turned up and arrested them all. As a result, the Internet connection in the bank lobby was switched off for two weeks. An argument at the bank meant no more research for Rafid.

Like all of us, he had no idea how to use a computer at first. We'd never seen one before, and the Internet seemed to us like a genie, a magical spirit in a bottle that could call up information from anywhere in the world. So the first few times, Rafid went to the bank with a friend who knew a bit more about these things. He explained everything to Rafid until he was able to search for names and dates on his own. The biggest problem was that the computer didn't have an Arabic keyboard. This meant that Rafid had to look for one online first, write the word in Arabic, copy it and then open the search engine, enter the word and press 'Search'.

Frau Schulz, you can imagine how long he had to stand around at that Internet point. He sometimes had to wait for one or two hours until the other users had finished and he could begin his search. However, it was never long before other interested people came into the bank and started queuing up behind him. Naturally, this put him under pressure. He tried to do it all as quickly as possible, skim-reading the text on the screen and noting down the most relevant details by hand. Searching for a single historical event might mean spending half a day in the bank lobby, most of it taken up with waiting.

He couldn't afford to have his own Internet connection because of the high monthly charges. It wouldn't have been allowed, anyway. Rafid asked a social services official if he could help him get an Internet connection, only to be told that it was too big a luxury for 'a homeless person on a stay of deportation', so no, he couldn't help him.

Rafid got hold of a free second-hand computer, though—not from social services but from me. I managed to fish one out of a skip while I was working at the recycling centre and smuggle it away. Unfortunately, the thing was louder than a vacuum cleaner and slower than a tortoise. Neither was it installed with word-processing software or an Arabic keyboard. In the end, Rafid handwrote everything. Even then, his notebooks came from me or, to be precise, from the recycling centre.

Rafid's asylum application was rejected six months after 9/11, and his life took a sudden and disastrous turn for the worse. All despite being probably the only one in the asylum hostel who had genuinely been in political trouble back home. He always claimed that telling the judge the truth had been his greatest mistake. What truth did he mean? No one knew any details.

He was only given a stay of deportation. He was forced to move into the homeless hostel and wasn't able to do anything but get bored. He refused to give up, though, contacting a lawyer and trying to fight the verdict. He also took the job centre to court because he couldn't get a work permit. The cases dragged on for several months, and in the end he achieved nothing.

Even his attempts to pursue further studies failed, although he'd sent his bachelor's certificate from Baghdad University to the Bavarian qualification accreditation centre. He'd already completed four years of English literature and one year of German in Iraq, but only a year and a half of those studies were recognized. He still tried to enrol at Niederhofen University, but they wouldn't let him in because he didn't have a residence permit. Rafid's life had suddenly become a vicious circle of dead ends. He eventually became withdrawn and spent all his time writing.

He only went properly mad, however, in the months after the outbreak of the Gulf War. It happened one Sunday in midsummer. Rafid turned up outside a cathedral and, one after the other, hurled seven stones at the beautiful Episcopal church.

'The devil is hiding inside!' he called with every throw.

Passers-by shot anxious and bewildered glances at him. And what did he do? He strode as proudly as a medieval knight back to his hostel.

None of us understood why Rafid was hunting Satan in Bavaria—in your homeland of all places, *Frau* Schulz. That's because the stone-throwing ritual is essentially the goal of a Muslim's pilgrimage to Mecca. There is a stone column in Mina symbolizing the prince of darkness. The devout are supposed to pick up seven stones and then throw them at the column, and therefore at the devil.

Following that bizarre Sunday, Rafid lost at least ten kilos within a short time. He looked gaunt—nothing but skin and bones. His eyes had a crazy glint to them, as if they could see invisible figures. He became aggressive and scary. Two of our lot had particular cause for concern, as he had threatened to slit their throats. They told me that Rafid was suspicious of any compatriot in Niederhofen, claiming that they were spying for the great powers.

One afternoon, I paid him a visit in his room to discuss the many complaints about him that had reached my ears over the preceding days.

'Which powers do you mean?' I asked him.

'You wouldn't understand, Karim.'

'Then please help me to understand. I'm your friend.'

'They want to prevent me from recognizing the absolute truth about the universe.'

'But you were always against any form of absolutism.'

'I was blind, Karim, but you are still afflicted by the darkness in your hearts. If your heart is blind, even the keenest eye will not help you.'

'Who are the people trying to stop you?'

'They're everywhere.'

'Who are they? Tell me about them.'

'I can point them out. Let's go.'

I was surprised that he was willing to reveal his enemies to me; I hadn't reckoned with this. We went outside. He glanced distrustfully to the left and then the right, scanning the surroundings as if he were being persecuted. After half an hour's walk in silence we reached Niederhofen's pedestrian zone.

'Did you hear what that woman just said to me?' Rafid's eyes rolled back, as if he might fall unconscious at any second. He pointed to a blonde woman walking past us.

'What did she want? I wasn't paying attention.'

'"We're out to get you, Rafid." That's what she said. And this man here?'

'Which one?'

'The old man in the Bavarian hat. He said, "We know all about you."'

It was depressing to see him in this state and not to be able to help him. I thought it might be merely a phase and that would soon blow over. But it got worse, *Frau* Schulz.

One time he rang me in the middle of the night. 'I've made a discovery. Come around right away!' he said and hung up.

When I got there and entered his room I was appalled. Only the TV was on. Rafid had draped tissues and toilet paper over all the lights, bulbs, lamps, stove lights, electric switches and power sockets.

'What are you doing, Rafid?'

'Shhh!'

'What?'

'They're listening. They're watching us. They're spying on me.'

'Who the hell do you mean?'

'German intelligence, the CIA, Mossad and the Saudi al-Mukhabarat al-A'amah.'

'They're all listening in on you?'

'Yes.'

'Why? How come you're suddenly so important?'

'Because I know he's here. And soon the world revolution will begin.'

'You're talking rubbish.'

'Be patient and listen to me. You're very fidgety.'

'Okay, okay!'

He stared at me as if he'd turned into a different person. 'He's hiding in the Bermuda Triangle in the Caribbean. Countless ships and planes have vanished there, along with their entire crews. Nobody can explain it. I've recently become aware that the Bermuda Triangle is the Green Island on which Imam Mahdi is hiding.'

'Imam Mahdi?'

'Yes. Our liberator. Soon he will come and we will all live peacefully together. Even the sheep will stroll peacefully through the woods with the wolves.'

'Sheep and wolves?'

A serious thought intermittently crossed my mind that Rafid was taking the piss. He'd always known a lot about religion, but I hadn't realized he was a believer. Now, though, he went on and on about the saviour. Not about your Jesus, *Frau* Schulz, but about Imam Mahdi. He's very famous. The twelfth imam of the Shiites, he is alleged to have simply vanished in the ninth century. Since then we have awaited his return, when he will bring justice into the world and save mankind from evil.

'The devil plans his wars in three places—in the White House, the Knesset and the Saudi Mukhabarat's palace. That's because the Sunnis are afraid that when the imam appears, mankind will realize the falsehood of their beliefs. They deny that he will return. The Israelis are experts in the art of prediction. Theirs is the oldest religion, and everything is written in their books. They knew of Jesus before he was born; they knew about Muhammad too, and they know that Imam Mahdi will soon be here. They killed Jesus and fought the Prophet Muhammad and now they're trying to stop our saviour. The Americans don't want any rival powers: they want to rule the world alone. They know that the imam disappeared in Iraq and that he will reappear there too. They keep sending weapons and soldiers to hold him back. Every twelfth year the Americans invade Iraq because they know that our imam tries to come back every twelve years—in 1979, 1991 and 2003. Each time the Americans are there to prevent his return. But now we're developing a new plan: we're working to make sure the Americans don't come back to Iraq in 2015.'

'I'm not sure about that, Rafid.'

'It's true. And do you know why it's every twelfth year?'

'No, but—'

'Mahdi is the twelfth Shiite imam and he may only achieve his goals within a single year. The other eleven years are the years of the other imams. He will only be with us for one year, but in those twelve months he will save the world. For that to happen, though, he must come back to find a strong Shiite Iraq, for only then can he launch the universal uprising. But how's he supposed to do that if the Americans keep destroying Iraq? We must prevent the Americans from returning to Iraq in twelve years' time at all cost. It won't be an easy year, but this time we're going to be ready. Imam Mahdi has made contact with many people like me. We have to explain to everyone else where the devil is hiding. Only when our enemies lose their power will we finally achieve peace and calm across the universe.'

It was a very sad evening, *Frau* Schulz. I was totally exhausted. Rafid abruptly fell silent and went back to watching TV, as if I wasn't in the room. He didn't seem to get tired. He watched the night-time repeat of a nature documentary with avid concentration. He didn't react when I said goodnight and left his room.

For three weeks Rafid was caught up in his world of messages and the secret services. Every day he came up with a fresh apocalyptic theory. For example, for one whole week he was obsessed with numbers around town. He went searching for symbols and gave the scariest interpretations. He took line 12 back and forth for days, convinced that Imam Mahdi planned to meet him on that particular bus. He kept an eye on every house in the town centre with that number. He believed that women and men of the revolution lived in those buildings. Only in the Haitzinger Strasse did he pause outside number 24, which housed a brothel. He believed that this house of ill repute was merely a decoy, although two times twelve had a special significance: It was, he said, the headquarters, the heart of the imam's international movement in Germany. In truth, every number had suddenly taken on a myriad of possible meanings for Rafid. I couldn't keep up. I can only recall that seventeen was the number of the devil—maybe because Niederhofen police station is at number 17 on the main street.

Rafid insulted a lot of people during this time. He suspected a homeless Italian man from the hostel of being a German spy. Rafid nagged on at him until the Italian lost patience and decided to sort him out. He hammered on Rafid's door, yelling, 'Foreigners, go home!', which sent Rafid into hiding under his bed.

At some point I decided to put a stop to this circus. It was clear that Rafid was no longer his familiar lovable self, and that he would never be again. I went to Caritas and spoke to *Frau* Mohmadi.

The poor woman was beside herself. 'I know he needs help,' she told me. 'He turned up here recently, looking unwashed and in a wretched state. He said that he could translate or interpret for Caritas. He claimed he was fluent in twelve languages including Hebrew, Chinese and Russian. When I asked him how he suddenly came to speak all these languages, he answered that poetry had helped him. He'd taken several volumes of poems in various languages into the shower with him, and the writing, the letters and the stanzas were now flowing through his body and his soul. He said he could learn any language using that method.'

'I suggest that he be sectioned immediately.'

'That isn't possible. He has to ask for that to happen. We can only get involved if he commits a crime.'

And that's exactly what Rafid did. He came to the immigration office with a knife to kill you, *Frau* Schulz. Now you remember him, right? He thought that you'd passed on his files to al-Qaida and that as a result they'd blown up his whole family in Baghdad.

The psychiatrists regard Rafid as dangerous, and so they pump him full of drugs and have him under round-the-clock supervision. It wasn't easy to get an appointment to see him. Every time I rang up I got the same answer from the other end of the line: 'No visiting.'

For weeks I tried in vain. One day in October the doctor said that it might help if Rafid were gradually re-familiarized with the outside world. *Frau* Mohmadi from Caritas arranged for me to see him in the Mainkofen District Clinic in Deggendorf.

I arrived punctually for my appointment. A security guard escorted me from the reception to a large room. I waited there for a while until a young woman at last came to fetch me. She led me into a visiting room and then left. The room wasn't very big. I sat down at the only table and studied the painting on the otherwise bare white wall. It was Vincent van Gogh's *Twelve Sunflowers in a Vase*. I counted them several times.

Then someone forced the glass door open with their back. Rafid was pushed into the room in a wheelchair by a carer. She positioned him opposite me and then left us alone.

'Hello, my friend.'

Rafid didn't look at me. His eyes were focused on the window. His face was pale. A slight trembling in his hands. Deep, black circles around his eyes, as if he hadn't slept for days.

'It's me. Karim.'

Finally he stirred, but still he didn't look at me, only at the floor. His head rocked from side to side.

'Rafid. My dear brother.'

No response.

I couldn't hold back my tears, *Frau* Schulz. I got quickly to my feet and peered through the glass door at the white psychiatric world beyond. It was totally quiet. I'd always imagined that mental asylums were chaotic, deafening places, like asylum seekers' hostels. But how are madmen meant to perform their crazy acts if they're all drugged up like Rafid? I wiped the tears from my eyes and sat down at the table again.

'Would you like me to tell you what's been going on in our lives and in Niederhofen while you've been away? You've missed a lot of things, my friend.'

Silence.

'I'll start with our eternal nightmare—Iraq. Is that good?'

Silence.

'Saddam is still in hiding somewhere. Nobody knows where he is. Terrorists have flooded into the country from all over the world. The new politicians are arguing with each other and making the situation worse. None of the infrastructure is working. There are power cuts all the time, some lasting up to twenty-four hours. Dirty tap water, terrible medical care, unpredictable militias and explosions. Attacks and suicide bombers practically every day. And the Americans? They're caught up in a never-ending duel with their enemies. Do you remember how people would challenge someone to a fight when we were still at school and they'd arrange to meet outside? That's precisely what it's like now. Any politicians anywhere in the world who feel like beating someone up outside their borders come to Iraq. Saudis versus Iranians, democrats versus terrorists, Muslims against Christians, Turks versus Kurds, Saddam supporters against Saddam opponents. Everyone against everyone else. You were right, Rafid, I swear. If a war ever breaks out between aliens and earthlings, it'll take place in Baghdad. What a wonderful country we have, don't you think?'

Silence.

'We're having immense trouble in Germany right now. Count yourself lucky that you're safely inside this nuthouse at the moment, Rafid. The authorities are on the hunt for us. They say that there's no reason for us to stay in Germany because the Americans have brought democracy to our land. Lots of people have already received a revocation of their right to stay. Lawyers are making a killing with us. On the other hand, everything's become much easier for Saddam supporters. They're allowed to live here. So the Germans are chucking us out and letting the fascists in. The Baathists are like the Nazis who cleared off to Argentina loaded with gold and cash after the Second World War. Bavaria is like Argentina for Iraqi fascists.'

Silence.

'You're lucky, my dear Pencil! Health reasons make you undeportable. But sadly I have to leave. I received a revocation letter. I'm probably going to run away soon—to Finland, Canada or Australia, or maybe even to Fiji. We'll see what happens. First, I have to find a smuggler. Next week I'm going to go to Munich and stay at Salim's for a while. He just got back from Baghdad. He was so homesick that he absolutely had to visit his family, despite having the same old blue asylum seeker's passport with which he's allowed to travel to any country *excluding* Iraq. Even so, there are ways and means of entering the country on that passport, Rafid. Salim got a helping hand from some Iraqi Kurds living in Syria. He first flew to Damascus, where the Kurds gave him a piece of paper he could use to travel in and out of Iraq without having his passport stamped. It only cost fifty dollars. Officially he was only supposed to have been in Damascus, but in fact he'd been to Baghdad and back. Now he's back in Munich. He had some bad experiences in Baghdad. We'll see if he says anything about them while I'm staying at his place. He didn't want to talk about it over the phone, anyway. He's still just as quiet and calm as when you knew him. He's looking for a bride at the moment. I think it'll take him some time to find one. He's simply too shy. Such a silent person. The main thing is that he's fine. That's the most important thing.'

Silence.

The carer knocked and quickly opened the door. 'You have another five minutes.'

Silence.

'Okay, my friend. What else should I tell you? I don't know. Our lives in Germany end right here, right now—that's if they ever really got started. That's our fate, and there's nothing we can do about it. We're like the cheap, tacky foreign products you find at Aldi or Lidl. We're hauled here on trucks like bananas and cattle, then arranged, graded, divided up and sold on the cheap. What's left is thrown into the bin.

'I'm leaving now. Have a good rest, my dear Pencil. I hope we see each other again soon!'

Dear *Frau* Schulz, the first thing I did after leaving the psychiatric ward was to sit down. There were a few benches and a small fountain facing the main entrance. It was deserted: no mad people, no doctors and no other visitors. Not so much as a sparrow on the clinic roof or a lost cat in this clean, artificial oasis.

I was exhausted. On the one hand, I felt profoundly sad; on the other, I was glad that I had at least seen Rafid again. I smoked one cigarette after another, gazing up into the grey sky and weeping. I don't know how long I sat there. At some stage it began to rain, though, and my tears stopped of their own accord. I got up and walked to the station.

A week later I took the black rucksack I'd bought for my language course and packed a few clothes. I left everything else behind: the flat and the furniture I'd collected, my friends, my acquaintances, my colleagues, the Danube, the asylum seekers, the people of Niederhofen, the Bavarian police officers and the immigration office. I got on the train to Munich to see Salim.

That's it, *Frau* Schulz. That was my stay in Germany. I've lived here for three years and four months. In Dachau, in Zirndorf, in Bayreuth, in Niederhofen an der Donau and in Munich. A lot happened during that time, but nothing I'm proud of.

I'm still not a normal man. I still have these damn breasts. Know what? If I'd started working illegally earlier, I could probably have paid for the operation long ago. But that's me—an honest fool. All I've achieved is a gigantic pile of nothing. The only person rubbing his hands in glee is my smuggler, Abu Salwan.

Instead of going to university, I was in a homeless hostel, the Goethe Mosque and Enlil Centre. Instead of rubbing shoulders with students and professors, I hung out with criminals, fanatics and rent boys. And now? I'm right back where I started. Once more I have to use a trafficker to move on, and the whole pointless process begins all over again. What would you do in my shoes, *Frau* Schulz? I have no choice, even though this planet is huge. I couldn't stay in Baghdad, I'm not allowed to stay in Germany, so I'll take a punt on Finland. Who knows if I'll even make it to Finland. You can't trust these smugglers. After all, I didn't make it to France.

Or you know what? Actually, I just want to go home. I can't stand it any more. I'll roll us another joint, okay?